AN UNFORTUNATE WOMAN

BOOKS BY BARRY GIFFORD

Novels

An Unfortunate Woman
Landscape with Traveler
Port Tropique

Short Stories

The Tunisian Notebook
Francis Goes to the Seashore
A Boy's Novel

Non-fiction

Saroyan: A Biography *(with Lawrence Lee)*
The Neighborhood of Baseball
Jack's Book: An Oral Biography of Jack Kerouac
(with Lawrence Lee)
Kerouac's Town
Uncle Buck

Poetry

The Paris / Venice Poems
Beautiful Phantoms: Selected Poems 1968-1980
Chinese Notes
Lives of the French Impressionist Painters
Horse hauling timber out of Hokkaido forest
Poems from Snail Hut
Persimmons: Poems for Paintings
A Quinzaine in Return for A Portrait of Mary Sun
The Boy You Have Always Loved
Letters To Proust
Coyote Tantras
The Blood of the Parade
Selected Poems of Francis Jammes *(translations)*

Editor

Selected Writings of Edward S. Curtis

An Unfortunate Woman

A Novel by

Barry Gifford

Donald S. Ellis · Publisher · San Francisco

Creative Arts Book Company
1984

Published by Donald S. Ellis, San Francisco,
and distributed by Creative Arts Book Company.
For information contact:
Creative Arts Book Company
833 Bancroft Way
Berkeley, California 94710

ISBN 0-916870-73-1 (cloth)
ISBN 0-916870-74-X (pbk.)
Library of Congress Catalog Card No. 83-82560

Cover illustration by James Brill Adams.

The publication of this book was supported in part by a grant from the National Endowment for the Arts in Washington, D.C., a Federal Agency.

For Dorothy Marjorie Colby

What would happen if one woman
told the truth about her life?
The world would split open.
> —*Muriel Rukeyser*

The truth is bald and cold,
But that will hold.
> —*Emily Dickinson*

I have always been greatly attracted by the undiluted
female mind. And I mean the adjective "undiluted" for
I am not thinking of exceptional minds, like Cleopatra
or Mrs. Carlyle or Jane Austen or Virginia Woolf; I am
thinking of the "ordinary" woman, undistinguished,
often unintellectual and unintrospective. The minds of
most women differ from the minds of most men in a
way which I feel very distinctly, but which becomes
rather indistinct as I try to describe it. Their minds seem
to me to be gentler, more sensitive, more civilized. Even
in many stupid, vain, tiresome women this quality is
often preserved below the exasperating surface. But it is
not easy to catch or bring it to the surface. You can only
do so by listening to, and by being really interested in,
what they say.
> —*Leonard Woolf*

AN UNFORTUNATE WOMAN

Jake is in Tijuana and I'm alone in the apartment. I was overwhelmed again today by a feeling of utter hopelessness. If I had any money of my own I would have left Jake long ago. This latest scheme of his to sell stolen machinery in Mexico isn't going to work out; the Mexicans will cheat him or put him in jail or his "friends," the Dragulis brothers, will find a way to cut Jake out of his part of the deal. How could I wind up in this situation, without a cent, depending on a man like Jake LaPointe? Perhaps if I wrote it all out, from the beginning, it would make more sense to me. The answer has to be in there somewhere.

*   *   *

Where did the time go? Where did the time go? Here it's been fifty-eight years and there's so much to do and see, so much left to accomplish; it's terrible. It just went too fast, it just slipped away; thinking every year's going to be better than the next. Working towards something and not achieving it.

It goes back to when I was a little girl, going to the bank with my mother, holding her hand. It was in 1929, the rush on the banks, my mother knocking on the window and the man saying, "Come back tomorrow. Come back tomorrow and we'll have all the money, we've had such a run today, we're getting extra cash. Come back tomorrow." And that was the end, there was no tomorrow and my parents lost their life's savings. It occurred to me then, at six years old, that life was full of lies, of disappointment and lies.

After the crash my mother divorced my father. He was out of work but that wasn't it, the problem wasn't financial; it was his shenanigans, his carrying on with other women that made her do it. My mother was unhappy; she went to her father, my grandpa Boris, a man who was always impeccably dressed, with blue-grey eyes and a big long red mustache, always examining his heavy gold pocket watch, and he told her to come home, it would be all right, and she left my father.

This was in Chicago, Illinois. My mother was a brave woman, forthright in every way for those days. She was the first woman in

4

Chicago to bob her hair. She taught the men in her family how to drive a car. She always drove a car. She had a talent for the stage, for acting, she sang; but she opted for being a good housewife and mother.

My grandmother Eva remembered the great Chicago fire; she and my grandpa arrived in Chicago the year before. Eva was supposed to have married a man in Kiev, it was an arranged marriage: she, the daughter of a sugar mill owner, to another mill owner's son. There was a big wedding and the orchestra contracted to play at the wedding was led by my grandfather. My grandmother ran away with him on her wedding night. They fled Russia and settled in Constantinople, Turkey. Their first child, my aunt Lilia, was born there. She told me how fierce the Turks were, how my grandmother had to cover her face when she went out on the street. Grandpa Boris played violin in a Turkish orchestra. They saved their money and eventually emigrated to the new country, America, where they opened a candy store in Chicago.

They worked hard and bought a small house in the city. Eva made ties for department stores; at night Boris worked in a cannery. He told his wife and daughter: "Here you speak no Russian, you speak no German or Turkish; you speak English." A second daughter, my mother Rose, was born in Chicago. As soon as she was old enough to go out by herself she began to bring home stray animals, hiding them under the bed and feeding them candy from the store. They lived on Paulina Street in a neighborhood composed mostly of Irish families just over on the boat. Everybody took pride in scrubbing their front steps. My grandmother Eva was a hardworking little ninety-pound woman.

My grandparents had never been particularly religious people. They were Russian Orthodox, but in Chicago, living in this Irish neighborhood, Eva's best friend being her next door neighbor, a woman from Dublin, they became Catholics, and indoctrinated my mother with the Catholic religion. This neighbor woman had six sons, all good looking Irish boys, and as my mother was growing up she developed a crush on one of the brothers. He

5

became a streetcar conductor and used to give my mother free rides up and down the line. A good looking young Irish guy with blue eyes and red hair like my grandpa Boris.

My mother went to Catholic school, of course, the local academy for girls, but she hated it, she couldn't stand the rules, the confinement. She didn't like the food and she used to climb over the wall to get out and go buy a pickle, a big dill pickle for a penny. Rose was a natural beauty and she knew it. She used to spit on a red blanket and rub it on her cheeks because she had no rouge. Her older sister Lilia was not as fortunate, she wasn't very pretty, and my mother would steal Lilia's boyfriends from her.

One day Rose had a date with Lilia's boyfriend, an ice skating champion named Halverson; she borrowed one of Lilia's dresses and snuck out of the house down the alley to meet him. Who should she run into but Lilia, who made her undress right in the alley. Both sisters told me this story without rancor; even as girls they loved each other, they laughed about this kind of thing, it was all a game. But my mother was the forward one, the one that you really couldn't step on. She was a fighter.

When my father fell in love with her, Rose was seventeen years old. He was in the millinery business, a buyer for an English firm. Jack McCloud. He used to travel all over: Boston, New York, Chicago, Kansas City. He saw my mother in a store trying on hats, struck up a conversation and later sent her a hat in a big box, one that she had tried on and hadn't been able to afford. He must have been very charming because he was always a hit with the ladies, women loved him. Of all the McCloud brothers—there were seven, all born in London, England—Jack was the most dapper, the dandy. He was a fine dresser with impeccable manners, excellent taste in food, clothes, everything; and that beautiful English accent. He was ten years older than my mother.

While Jack McCloud courted my mother her father's health failed. They lived on the northwest side of town and it was at this time that a silk factory was built on the block next to my grandparents' house. I remember years later going over to visit and seeing a man fall from a scaffolding on the side of the factory to the sidewalk. He was dead as soon as he hit the ground and I watched the brains ooze from his head. Grandpa Boris hated the factory; he sued the company, tried to get them to move, but he was unsuccessful. The factory ruined the neighborhood, he said, it spoiled the looks of the street.

A woman named Jenny O'Leary lived across the street. She had a white spitz dog and became a drunkard after her husband left her. My mother was a good friend of hers and used to try to help her out. Jenny was a good looking gal who used to take in roomers, each of whom she had some kind of affair with until she threw them out. She'd go to my mother for consolation. "Get rid of them, Jenny," my mother would say, "you don't need them, they're just men!" But my mother had her own problems, of course, with my father, and she divorced him when I was seven.

I wasn't sure what had happened, only that my father wasn't home. One night I started to cry and couldn't stop. My brother Buck, who was nineteen, was away somewhere, my mother was busy with the church and I felt totally abandoned. My mother came in and found me clinging to this totally wet pillow, soaked with tears, and she tried to calm me. "Peggy, Peggy, stop, stop," she begged, but I was out of control. I don't know how long I wept, but when I did stop I felt alone, absolutely alone. Nothing could change it.

My mother married the streetcar conductor, her former next door neighbor, Dan O'Rourke, who had since divorced his first wife. O'Rourke, however, was no longer a streetcar conductor. He now worked with his brothers in the trucking business, distributing canned goods, and they were doing quite well. O'Rourke had caught his ex-wife with a policeman. I don't know how he met my mother again, or came in contact, but after my father moved out O'Rourke started coming around to the house, courting my mother and promising her the moon. My brother was in Alabama at this time, putting himself through college.

Buck came back to Chicago every now and then. He was a magician and he'd do his tricks for me and ask if anything showed. I always looked up to him because he was so handsome and kind. He had millions of girls running after him all the time, and he was adventurous, always full of great stories. His early life was difficult; my father and mother didn't pay a great deal of attention to him and let him fend for himself. My dad would give Buck a dollar and say run along, and take my mother out on the town. He didn't get the right kind of attention from his parents, although they did love him. My father travelled quite a bit, so he wasn't always around, and my mother used to make Buck scrub the floors and clean in the corners with a knife. He sold newspapers on the street and I remember seeing him standing on the corner with his papers while I sat with my mother in her big beige car with the window shades.

By the age of twelve Buck was in business for himself. An uncle of ours had a novelties and jewelry business and Buck learned about it from him. Buck took out ads in magazines and newspapers and one day a man came to our door and asked to see Mr. McCloud. My mother said that he was at work. "Mr. William McCloud?" said the man. (William is Buck's real name, but no one who knows him calls him anything but Buck.) My mother called Buck down from upstairs and the man was shocked to see that the owner of the Washtenaw Novelty House was a twelve year old boy!

Of course this was before I was born, my mother told me about Buck's businesses as a boy. Soon after she had my brother, my mother fell ill in the street with rheumatic fever. It severely affected her heart and she was never the same after that. She always felt sick and wasn't sure what was wrong with her, but it was her heart, the valves were damaged. Eventually she got anemia and then a stricture of the esophagus. She had been a champion ice skater, roller skater and high diver, and within a few years of my birth she couldn't do much anymore, she was too sick. Her sister Lilia married a jeweler and the girls remained very close. Lilia helped Rose and was always good to me.

Buck was not welcomed by Dan O'Rourke, a fact that my mother did not realize at first. We moved from the city to Prairie Park, a well-to-do suburb west of Chicago. My mother's heart gave her trouble and she grasped at the Catholic church; she began to devote most of her time to the church. I was sent to Catholic school.

My stepfather was the most irreligious Catholic I have ever known. He was a man of spartan habits. He would rise at five in the morning and go directly to the basement, where he had constructed a gymnasium, and work out for one hour before sitting down to breakfast. My mother was an excellent cook, and

9

she insisted on preparing all of the family meals herself despite the fact that she always had help in the house. It was a large house with twenty-two steps from the first floor to the second. We had half an acre and my mother grew her own vegetables. Buck built a star rock garden in the yard and put in a fountain with an angel holding a fish out of whose mouth the water spouted. O'Rourke was never very kind to Buck, however, and never gave him any money to help him through college. He put himself through school because our father was in tough financial shape at the time.

My father had moved to Kansas City, where his only sister lived. He went into the fur business after the British millinery outfit shut down. His father had apparently been a furrier in London but had become an alcoholic and did nothing for many years. My father's mother was from Spain and she raised her sons without much help from her husband, whom my father always described as worthless. The sons stuck together in the United States, eventually establishing a flourishing fur business in Chicago. All of them were great jokers, with marvelous high spirits and generous natures. My father was the gadabout, the gay blade, but the brothers were great friends to the end.

My mother's family came to visit us often, probably because they never went away from our house empty-handed. They always went home with grocery bags filled with canned goods and homemade pies and cakes. They all blamed my mother for the divorce from my father, except for one, my Aunt Maria. Maria and her husband Bill both graduated from Northwestern University and moved to New York. They were quite well-to-do, having made their money in Chicago real estate. They owned a number of fine clothing stores in the Loop, and I remember riding down State Street with them in their chauffeur-driven limousine. Uncle Bill was killed in a car wreck when he was in his mid-forties, leaving each of his two daughters a million dollars apiece and several millions to my Aunt Maria. In New York Maria supported starving artists, actors and writers, helping them through school. One of her great projects was Johnny Weissmuller, the Olympic

10

swimming champion who became an actor, known best for his portrayal of Tarzan. In her later years Maria opened up a swanky milk farm, a reducing villa, where rich women came to lose weight. She was quite a woman, very independent. She never remarried.

Maria was a good looking woman, a brash sort who wore her long gray hair piled up on top of her head, with sharp black eyes and sparkling white teeth. She was extremely bright and a hard one to fool. Her mother had the same natural beauty but Maria had the oomph to go with it. That Aunt Maria. She really was a marvelous businesswoman. I was in high school when she opened a reducing villa in Chicago and I used to go there with a girl friend. Of course we didn't have to lose weight but we'd go for a weekend and have some fun, take a pair of beds in one of the dormitories and sneak down at night and eat ice cream when nobody else was around. We'd raid the refrigerators. It was a fabulous place and we'd see the different movie stars and entertainers who came there to get in shape, to relax or diet. There were masseurs, hair dressers, swimming instructors, everything. It was on the lake and we'd go rowing and have a great time.

Once we moved to Prairie Park my life changed. I had been a sickly child, and I blossomed in the country, drinking good milk and eating eggs right from the farms. My mother had a lady friend who raised rabbits; she gave some to me and I kept them, too. On Friday nights my mother always had a party, she'd entertain for a dozen or more people. This became a ritual, and I would sit on the stairway and look through the wooden bars at all the nice company. And my mother was a fancy cook. At Christmas time she'd work for days preparing foods, ice cream molds and butter made into the shape of a deer. She delighted in this kind of thing. She really fussed an awful lot. She and Dan had their ups and downs. I don't think she was really very happy with him, he turned out to be not a very intelligent or open-minded man. It upset my mother that he didn't want Buck around, and that he seemed to care little for me.

11

Dan wasn't cruel to me; he was really a nonentity insofar as I was concerned. He hated my dog, Toy, a big chow. He was mean to animals, he thought their only purpose was as watchdogs. My mother, though, continued to pick up stray animals of all kinds, and this used to drive Dan crazy. He'd beat Toy with a wire hanger because he knew Toy disliked him. I'd go into a closet and hide when he did this, it made me sick. Toy lived outside. He would roll in the snow and sleep on the porch during the winter, which didn't bother him because of his thick red fur coat. He'd kill anything that wandered into the yard, any cat or strange dog or raccoon. Toy was a fierce animal, a marvelous watchdog who would attack any human being if he thought they might harm me.

Dan O'Rourke didn't speak often. He'd come home and read his paper and have his dinner and go for his ride in the country on Sundays. He was insanely jealous of any man who paid the slightest attention to my mother. I think he really did make her life miserable in that respect. I had no affection for O'Rourke and can honestly say that I felt nothing one way or another when he died, which was only four or five years after he married my mother. I don't remember my mother mourning very much at his death, she had the church, and it didn't seem to make much of an immediate difference in our lives.

When we lived in Prairie Park I boarded at Catholic school. My mother liked the training of the sisters and it was an honor for the Mother Superior to visit the house, which she often did. My mother joined the church choir and was quite popular, though there was much jealousy in the neighborhood. We had the largest house on the block, and there were those, I'm sure, that felt my mother was stand-offish, which she was when she didn't like someone's looks. She had excellent taste and made sure that everything was kept just so.

I remember the dark raisin carpeting, which was so hard to keep clean, and the heavy red brocade drapes, the gold silk papering on the walls in the upstairs reading room. There was a small nook off the kitchen with a padded seat, just large enough to hold one person on each side. There was a wall of books there and I loved to curl up in the nook and read. That was my spot in the house, I loved it. My mother would come in and say, "Why don't you go outdoors and play? Get some color in that pale skin." Nobody would believe me, looking at me today, that I was puny and had long, skinny legs; I certainly wasn't very attractive. My skin was sallow, very pale, and I had chestnut red hair with freckles on my nose. But after a time in Prairie Park I became a tomboy. I loved to climb the cherry trees in our yard and to pick up snakes like the boys and run after girls to frighten them. Like I say, I did blossom.

I had a secret crush on a next door neighbor, Tommy White. He was a few years older than I was, and he liked my girl friend, who looked like Jean Harlow. When Jean Harlow died my friend almost died! Tommy White asked my friend out on a date and I couldn't wait until I saw her the next day to find out what had happened. I went over to see Marguerite—we thought it providential rather than coincidental that our names were practically the same: Marguerite and Margaret, though everyone called me Peggy—first thing in the morning and found her in tears. Tommy had tried to rape her and Marguerite's father was threatening to call his lawyer. That was the end of my crush on Tommy White; it was disgusting. Of course I didn't even know what rape meant, but I knew it must be something bad to have affected Marguerite the way it had. I was very sheltered.

I had another friend across the street, Edna Hudson, a fat, blonde girl with beautiful smooth white skin. My mother was friendly with her mother, though I remember Dan O'Rourke saying to her, "How can you associate with that woman? She likes to stand up on her porch without any pants on under her dress and let the men look at her!" These things that I remember! But Lucille Hudson was a nice woman whose husband owned a Mohawk gas station in town. He was handsome and Lucille adored him, but he ran away with another woman. It was like Peyton Place, that Prairie Park.

Dan would make beer and root beer in the basement, and I liked to lie in bed on warm summer nights and listen to the corks pop; it gave me a good feeling. I had a little room upstairs, with two closets under the eaves, and I'd look out over the whole backyard. It was so beautiful in the springtime, all filled with flowers. My brother kept the hull of a boat in the alley behind the yard, and whenever he came home he worked on it. Buck was going to build his boat and sail away forever and become another Jack London. That's what he would tell me.

After Dan died Buck came home more often. I loved him and admired him so much. For a while he wanted to be a taxidermist. In his closet he had stuffed snakes and squirrels and I couldn't

14

wait until he left the house so that I could sneak into his room and explore. His room was much larger than mine and he had about twenty-five pictures on the wall over his bed, all of beautiful girls. The girls he took out, not magazine pin-ups. Girls kept sending him pictures. God, he was so handsome! He was quite a guy.

I remember him taking me to the movies, at the Peacock Theater, not too far from Prairie Park, on a night they had a Clark Gable look-alike contest. We were stopped in the lobby of the theater and a man offered to send Buck to Hollywood for a screen test, which he refused. Buck had two giant dimples in his cheeks, and one in his chin. Later on he grew a mustache which made him resemble Douglas Fairbanks.

Buck always worked hard. His goal in life was to make a lot of money, and he did, but he didn't hoard it or spend it all on himself; even when he was very young he was generous with money and his possessions. My mother never really knew what Buck was up to, and once when she and my father went to the theater they were surprised to be seated by their own son, who was working as an usher. He had so many jobs, always trying different things. People were charmed by him, you couldn't help but like him.

Years later, when times were rough, Buck was in a CCC camp in Wisconsin, and he would buy food for all the boys. We went up to see him, my mother and I. It was snowing, and he showed us his pet deer, Peggy. Oh, she was so sweet. And then somebody poisoned her. Instead of being furious, Buck cried; he loved her so and had named her after me. He didn't get angry, he accepted it; my strange and wonderful brother.

Dan O'Rourke's father was half Scotch, on his mother's side, and he was not a Catholic; he didn't like the Catholics, though of course his wife was a devout one. She was the boss of that family, and when the old man died, old James O'Rourke, she made sure he was given a Catholic burial. The O'Rourkes were a socially-conscious bunch, members of a country club, all that. They had a daughter who married into society, a gorgeous girl named Megan. Old Mrs. O'Rourke was good to my mother, she liked her because she thought my mother was classy; the O'Rourkes were very concerned with status and getting ahead in the world. It seemed that everyone I knew in those days was socially aware, wanting to improve their station; they cared so much about what other people thought.

My father never lost track of us. He wrote to my mother during the years they were divorced, telling her he still loved her, that he had been wrong, asking her to take him back. Sometimes when he would come to Chicago from Kansas City or wherever he'd been he would stand across the street from our house and watch for my mother to come out. This was while my mother was still married to Dan. Rose would correspond with Jack only through me. I don't know if he supported me during this time but he'd always send things, worthwhile presents: the best sweaters, candies, books; even little white mice!

When I got old enough to travel alone I'd go to Kansas City on my school vacations and visit him. This didn't always work out so well, however, because I didn't like his girl friends. He had the tawdriest looking girl friends! I vaguely remember his second wife, a blonde, fast type. All of his women friends were floozies, especially that wife. His second marriage lasted barely a year; it ended when I was there, with her trying to scratch his eyes out. It was quite a scene and I was glad when it was over because she left. I was twelve years old then.

On that same trip to Kansas City my father and I went to a movie—we spent a lot of time going to movies, restaurants and even night clubs, sometimes—and I noticed a man staring at me. I wondered why he was staring at me and then I noticed that my new little breasts were showing through my thin summer dress. I was horrified and embarrassed and thought that I should bind myself up so that nobody could ever get a look at me! I'd stay at my aunt's house in Kansas City, too, my father's sister's place. One time my dad and I went out on the town, to dinner and a club. I had a great time, and then came back to my aunt's house and threw up in her bed all over her fine satin covers. I felt so guilty about that! To think that I'd given her so much work, so much trouble. I think I've always had a guilt complex about putting people out, causing them problems. Anyway, I felt terribly about it—I guess I still do!

After Dan died my mother got a little money, not very much really, and the house. She was getting weaker and weaker due to pernicious anemia and her heart condition. My father began to come around more often then and begged her to go back with him. He courted her all over again and they eventually remarried. I was happy about this. They were married very quietly and he came to live in our house in Prairie Park.

For some reason, though, the neighbors began to give my mother a hard time. She got crank phone calls and I don't know what else happened. These small-minded, suburban people didn't like the idea of my mother remarrying my father so soon after Dan O'Rourke's death. I can't remember how long an interval there was between his death and the marriage but whatever the period it wasn't long enough for those meddlers. Women called her a floozy when they saw her on the street; it really was an awful situation. So my mother decided to sell the house and move back into the city.

That was a wonderful time. At first we stayed in a hotel in Chicago and went out for dinner all the time and to nightclubs. My father really was a fine dresser and a smooth talker and got along well with everyone. My mother was too weak to carry on all the time, of course, so often my dad would take me out—I was fifteen, then—and introduce me to the club owners and restaurant owners and various men and women about town. What I didn't know at the time was that he was breaking me in for my first marriage, showing me the world, the night life and high roller types that I would soon come to know all too well.

My dad didn't have a cruel bone in his body, he was a nice guy; he was just wayward, I guess, when it came to women. He just had that thing about him. He was different than the other brothers; not that he wasn't a hard worker, he was, but he loved to dress up, to look good. His clothes came first. And he liked his family to be that way, too, to look good. He was attractive and attracted to women, who always gave him a second look. Jack McCloud really cut a figure in Chicago in those days—this was in the '30s—he was on a first name basis with the maitre d's of all the best restaurants. He always had a smile and a good word, people liked him.

Rose sold the house at the wrong time, though, before the Second World War, when prices zoomed. She actually came out with not very much from the sale; if she'd kept it another five years she could have tripled it. She gave the money to my father who opened up his own fur shop in the heart of the Loop. My parents bought a house on the North side, in partnership with my Aunt Lilia and her husband. When I graduated from school my father threw a grand party at Big Jim Colosimo's place. The entire family was there, sitting at tables up close to the runway—this was a night-time party—so that we could see all the half-naked ladies prancing around. This was a great time in my life.

18

I never knew my father's parents. All I know is what I learned from photographs and the little my mother mentioned about what he told her. I never really knew much about them except that the old man was supposed to have been a terror, a drunk who bullied his wife and the children. How his sons and daughter turned out so well I don't know, but they did. None of them spoke much about their father, and the only impression I had of him was that he sat around with his whiskey bottle while the old lady scrubbed the floors and cleaned and did everything. My father apparently contributed the most to his parents' upkeep; he and my uncles supported them until they died. My dad may have been something of a roué, running around with all these ladies, spending his money on them, but he did make sure the family's bills were paid.

My brother Buck got into a jam when he was about twelve or thirteen years old, and had to be rescued by my mother. Buck had saved money from his newspaper job and the novelties business and he fell in with a bad bunch of boys. He gave them fifty dollars or so to buy a car so that they could all run away from home. These boys were quite a bit older than Buck, sixteen or seventeen, I guess, and they bought a roadster with his money. According to my mother, she got a phone call from one of the other kids' mothers who had overheard a conversation her son had had with another boy. Apparently these boys were going to rob my brother of the rest of his money and then throw him out along the way. They were actually planning to murder Buck. My mother found out where they were and chased them down, nipped the thing in the bud and somehow managed to get Buck's fifty dollars back. My father used to love to tell this story, to tell how bold my mother had been. "They were really going to *kill* Buck!" he'd say. "But Rose stopped them."

After we moved back to the city I went to a coed school for the first time in my life. Public high school was a shock. I was awed by the whole thing, just awed. I felt so alone; I didn't make friends easily. I used to look at the girls and I'd think, how beautiful they are, not yet realizing that I, too, was blooming. In class one day one of the teachers, a woman, looked at me and said, "You're changing Peggy; you're looking so beautiful, just like your mother." Before this people had always said to me, "Oh, you'll never be as pretty as your mother. She's really something."

But my mother was ill, her health seriously declined after the move from Prairie Park. My children never knew her as she was. My son remembers her as old and in miserable health, unhappy and bedridden, which is so sad; she really was quite a doer, a talented and beautiful woman before her heart condition became so debilitating. She used to cry because she missed her gardens in Prairie Park; she hated the cement yard in Chicago. She began to have strokes, and couldn't walk properly. She'd bump into walls and say, "I know it's there but I can't turn." My father tried to persuade her to go into a sanitarium for a year, to get her proper rest, but she wouldn't do it; she had to be around for me, she said.

I did all right in school. I liked French, but more than anything I enjoyed reading books, getting away in my own dream world. I didn't like what I saw happening around me all the time, the petty social snobbery, the way people talked and acted. Not the kids my own age but older people; the world frightened me. I didn't like all the dishonesty, the put-on airs, the dissension; I just couldn't stand it. I hated it when people argued, I'd run away and hide. I had a nervous condition that came out all over me, literally, with eczema. I was born with that curse. I grew up with bandages on,

20

often from head to foot. One thing I welcomed in Catholic school was being able to hide my sore-ridden arms under the long sleeves of the uniform. My mother spent years dragging me to doctors, trying to help me. Once I had so many x-rays that my neck turned black, and the boys used to rib me about it. "Don't you ever wash your neck?" they'd say, and I'd cringe; it hurt me so.

I had eczema so badly as a child that I'd bleed. My grandmother would try the old country remedies on me. She'd take a leaf from a plant and bandage my arm with it, or soak a rag in cold milk and bathe me. In the winter my mother would take me to Florida, to see if the change of climate would help my skin condition. We'd go on the train, and riding through Georgia we'd see convicts in their striped outfits working in chain gangs with pickaxes. I'd be afraid to look at them, afraid one of them would hit me with an axe. How silly I was; these poor guys looking at all of these wealthy people on a train, sitting in the parlor cars, sipping their coffee and tea. I had no idea of what the world was really like. My father always liked to see us go first class, he was that type of man. I could see how sorry he felt for me, his poor little daughter bandaged up, in pain. I remember how I loved riding in the train, watching the countryside pass by, feeling that I really didn't belong to any of it, to the world at all. Nothing seemed real, Peggy McCloud didn't exist; it was all a dream. My mother always had her little flask full of whiskey to help her go on, to help her heart, and the smell of that mixed with everything. Such a strange, frightened child I was. I felt so helpless.

I didn't make many friends in Chicago; I wanted to, but I was shy. After awhile I met a boy named Hal French, a handsome, well-mannered guy, just the type of fellow every daughter's mother would be happy to have around. Hal was the school ROTC leader and a great athlete, and he became my boyfriend for the last three years of high school. There was never any doubt in Hal's mind that we'd be married someday. He was going to be an engineer and he did become one, but I don't know what happened between us. I suppose my image of Hal was as a schoolboy, and I went looking for something else. Who knows?

Hal looked up to my brother, too; and if my girlfriends found out that Buck was home they'd put on lipstick and fix their hair and run right over to my house. All the girls loved Buck. A woman came up to my mother in a department store one day and told her she'd like me to model clothes for her at Marshall Field's, so I began doing that, and Buck used to tell his buddies that his little sister was a fashion model in Chicago.

Modelling wasn't going to be a career, my mother didn't want that for me, but it brought in a few extra dollars. Buck used to make me walk with a book on my head to improve my posture. I was unusually tall for my age and already had a good figure; in fact I was always on the thin side, which is hard to believe, looking at me now. When I married Rudy, my first husband, he'd always say, "God, I wish you'd gain some weight in the rear."

One day after I'd finished a modelling job my mother and I stopped in a restaurant to have a bite to eat. It was more of a cafeteria-type place, where people sat at each other's tables, shared tables, and the place was crowded. A nice-looking man sat down with us; I imagine at the time that he must have been in his late thirties. I was fourteen or fifteen, and my facial complexion was uncommonly clear; I never did have a pimple, only the recurrent eczema, which wasn't bothering me at this particular time. This gentleman started a conversation with my mother. He was very friendly and kept looking over at me and smiling. He found out where I modelled, and when, and the next time I worked he showed up. Afterwards he invited my mother and me to dinner, an invitation she accepted.

At dinner he told me that he was from New York and was the owner of the largest car rental firm in this country. He wanted to make a bargain with my mother. "I know your daughter is very young now," he told her, "but I want to marry her. I'm willing to wait until she's seventeen or eighteen or however old you say." That's what he said, I'll never forget it. Of course my mother thought that this was an absurd situation, but he offered to support me, to support my mother and father, until I was old enough to marry him. He was very flattering, and in the succeeding weeks and months he tried to buy me everything I could possibly want. He sent me presents all the time, and took me to the movies, along with my mother, of course, as chaperone. He had dark, curly hair and his teeth came out a little in the front. I remember going to the movies and his wanting to hold my hand, but I wouldn't even sit next to him. When I had to go to the bathroom I excused myself and I purposely, with all my might, stepped on his feet walking to the aisle. I don't know why my mother allowed his pursuit of me to go on as long as it did. One time I came out of school and there was a limousine idling in the street. The chauffeur came up to me and said, "You don't have to take the street car, young lady. It's all arranged by Mr. So-and-so." I just took off, ran to my girlfriends and wouldn't accept the ride.

That night I told my mother I wouldn't go along with it anymore, I wouldn't see that man again; and that ended it.

It was this kind of thing, though, fine restaurants, big cars, big money, that impressed me, even if I was frightened by the men who could provide it. Poor Hal French and the other high school boys didn't really have a chance at that point. As soon as these older men started running after me things changed. I was scared but intrigued, and I knew I'd have to see it through, to satisfy my curiosity.

I didn't know very much about sex in those days, nothing for *sure*. I'd never seen a naked man until I was about ten or eleven when my friend Edna Hudson and I spied on my stepfather one night while he was doing his exercises in the basement. Actually it was something of an accident that we saw him because we were following a snake, a long garter snake along the side of the house to where it dipped out of sight into a drain next to the window. I never thought about the symbolism of it before, seeing the snake and it leading us to the naked man, but that's what happened. Dan was doing his knee bends in the nude and Edna and I were shocked at the sight of him.

Not long after this I frightened our maid, Floss, by taking a big light bulb, dressing up like a man and sticking the bulb under my pants like a penis and sticking it out at her! She told my mother and I was scolded, of course, but it was great fun. That was the summer I got scarlet fever and was quarantined in my room. This was still in Prairie Park. I'd lie in bed and fantasize that I was a great artist, that I could paint and draw like my father could; he used to sit and paint my mother's portrait and other things—I don't have any idea what happened to those paintings, they all disappeared. It's too bad because he was a good artist. I'd started playing the piano at that time and I'd fantasize that I was a great concert pianist, or a jazz singer, a singer like my mother could have been.

My mother told me that one night she was singing in her father's candy store, in the back where grandpa Boris would hold his impromptu musicales, and a man came in, presented his card, and said that he was a talent scout for Florenz Ziegfeld. He wanted to take Rose and train her for the theater, to pay my grandparents fifty dollars a week and the same to Rose, which was a great deal of money in those days. My grandmother chased him out of the store with a broom! Go on the stage? Why, that was unheard of in a respectable family To wear make-up? A horrible thing. And so on. So my mother was frustrated in her early life by that kind of closed-minded attitude.

I tried to sing but I wasn't as talented as my mother. She'd try to coach me a little, but she knew I didn't have it. I couldn't really draw, either, at least not well enough to justify an attempt to develop what little talent I did have. I could play the piano all right, and I'd make my scrapbooks and cut out pictures by the hour, and sit and read. I really was a loner; I had friends but I enjoyed being by myself. I was so shy that I didn't know how to properly acknowledge a compliment; I'd just blush and look away. My brother saw this and decided that I should go to finishing school in Lake Forest, to Faerie Hall, to learn how to take care of myself so that I'd be able to marry the right man and have a good, secure life. Buck really tried to look out for me. "My god, she's so sheltered," he'd tell my parents. "Let's get Peggy out into the world."

But I came down with another vicious attack of eczema just after I graduated from high school. That set me back for several months. Buck was becoming a flier in the Air Corps at Randolph Field in Texas by this time and he told my parents to ship me down to Austin, to the University of Texas, and he promised to keep an eye on me.

I loved going to the football games; I loved having hot chili after the games on Saturday. I was in awe of these big guys wearing boots and cowboy hats. I roomed with a pretty blonde girl from Dallas whose father was in the cotton gin business.

26

There were so many pretty blonde girls down there, all as fast as could be. And I didn't even know what a douche bag was! I had no idea. It turned out that I was allergic to cosmetics, and to fingernail polish, which I had never used until my roommate gave me some. I started rubbing my eyes because of the allergy and pretty soon I lost my eyelashes, all of them. Buck always used to say, "Peggy's got the most beautiful eyelashes. Look at those long, gorgeous lashes." Well, I lost them. I rubbed and rubbed my eyes and the school doctor gave me allergy tests. One week he forbade me to eat chicken, another week to drink milk, and so on. They tried different things, not knowing that it was the eczema again, creeping up into my face and eyes.

So I suffered with the allergies and eczema but I had a good time, too. I took two cow's eyes out of the formaldehyde in a biology lab and put them on a girlfriends's dinner plate, under her napkin, and when she picked up the napkin she got the fright of her life! She wouldn't talk to me for a few days after that. I did some crazy things and enjoyed myself.

I remember the beautiful chimes in the tower playing "The Eyes of Texas Are Upon You," they played it every day at noon; this is the tower from which years later a fellow shot several people. I have a picture of myself standing under it. In those days I wore saddle shoes and bobby socks, and long hair. It got very cold in the winter, we didn't have central heating, of course, and the bad weather seemed to aggravate my skin condition. It got so bad that I was forced to leave school and return to Chicago. My mother took me to an eye specialist who told me to remove the nail polish and gave me eyedrops and some ointment. I really thought I was going blind, but he assured me that I had 20/20 vision and that I would be all right.

I had the doctor's prescriptions filled at the drugstore on the corner of Rush and Chicago streets, which in those days was a very busy place, the center of the club district. Showgirls from the Club Alabam next door were bustling in and out and there were all sorts of strange, flashy characters standing around talking or chewing on cigars. I became friendly with the pharmacist, since I had to visit the doctor, whose office was nearby, several times, and to have the prescriptions filled. When I went back to school in Texas the pharmacist sent me presents from the store: perfumes and powder, things like that. I used to give it all to my girlfriends because I couldn't use them. I told him that but he continued to send me things anyway, just to stay in touch.

I stayed at Texas for one more year. I didn't want to go to school anymore, it didn't interest me. In fact, I didn't know what was going on half the time. I was out of place, things were going right by me; I felt lost and alone, isolated. I made good grades, but I don't know where my mind was. It all felt wrong somehow, so I left. I was actually frightened of everything and everybody, I'm still not sure why. I was nineteen years old.

My brother had gotten married when I was fifteen. He was in the Navy and stationed at Parris Island, South Carolina. Buck and his wife, Laura Mae Allen—she was from Savannah, Georgia—had a house in Beaufort, and my mother and I took a bus down there in June, a month after the wedding. Beaufort was just beautiful, with Spanish moss hanging down and picturesque little country lanes. My sister-in-law, Laura Mae, was quite happy to see us, but the trip was a hardship on my mother. She stayed in Beaufort about a week and then returned to Chicago. I stayed on, at Laura Mae's request, for the rest of the summer.

I learned the art of crabbing down there; it was my favorite pastime. I'd go down to the water with a big, high tall basket and a piece of suet and let it down into the water and wait for the crab to walk into it. I learned the markings so that I wouldn't catch any female crabs—which was against the law, I believe—and pretty soon, in a few hours, the basket would be filled. I'd take it home and give it to the big black cook in the kitchen who would make all of these fabulous dishes.

I pretended I was sixteen—I looked older, anyway—so that I could associate with the young Navy fliers and their girlfriends. These people were twenty, twenty-one or twenty-two, the children of old time Navy people who had travelled everywhere. One girl I knew had been born in the Sahara desert; another was born in Peking. They were service brats. We'd drive into Savannah for a mint julep, which was a great thrill for a fifteen year old girl! But I got away with it. I dated a few of the fliers. My brother would allow me to stay up until 11:30. I could invite my date to sit on the porch with me and have one cigarette, then he'd have to leave. I was having a high old time. My idyll ended when September came and I had to go back to school in Chicago; then everyone found out how young I was. Every one of those fliers I dated that summer was killed in the war. One boy, Tommy Lamarr, made a lasting impression; maybe because of his name, since Hedy Lamarr was such a popular actress in those days. Tommy was so beautiful, a sweet southern boy with big black eyes. He was usually my escort at the dances, when the "Beer Barrel Polka" was number one on the hit parade. Tommy was a smooth dancer, a swell guy, and when Buck told me years later that he'd been killed I couldn't believe it. All of that time seems like a dream to me now.

The summer that I was sixteen I worked as an assistant to the director of the San Carlos Opera Company. The director was a friend of my mother's; he would dictate to me in a heavy Italian accent, always with a blue beret on his head. He never dictated without that beret on. I'd have to make his imperfect sentences into understandable English. It was fun for me, I made some money and got to meet many of the great opera stars of the day. One of them, whose name I've now forgotten, noticed me staring at him in awe and said, very gently, "Do close your mouth, young lady." That job and modelling were the only two types of work I had until many years later.

My high school boyfriend, Hal, went into the Navy following graduation; he was stationed on the lake front in Chicago. Every Sunday night we'd meet and have dinner at Rickett's, which was right around the corner from the pharmacy where I'd gone to have my eye-drop and ointment prescriptions filled. Once in a while Hal and I would drop into the drugstore and I'd say hello to Rudy, the pharmacist who'd been so nice to me. Rudy was about twenty years older than I was, a stocky, powerfully built man of average height. Rudy was not very good looking but, as I say, he was extremely nice and helped me out.

One evening I was standing on the corner of Chicago and Rush waiting for Hal when I heard a car horn tooting and tooting. I turned around and saw a Cadillac at the curb, filled with sailors.

At the wheel was Rudy, the pharmacist. I didn't recognize him at first and turned away, paying them no attention. Rudy got out of the car and came up to me and started a conversation. As soon as I saw that it was Rudy I got very friendly and he asked me if I'd like to come along with him and the boys and have something to eat. I told him that I was waiting for my date and just then Hal came up. "Oh, is this your date?" Rudy said, and Hal said hello to him. It turned out that they knew each other, or at least Hal knew who Rudy was; as I was to find out very shortly, everybody who had any business in that part of town knew Rudy, from the high to the low. Rudy Winston was a popular figure in the club district.

"Well," said Rudy, "can I treat you kids to something? Do you want to come along? I'm just giving these sailors a lift out to the Great Lakes Naval base." We told him no, that we had a time limit because Hal had to be back on duty soon, and that was the end of it. The next day I got a phone call from Rudy. He'd gone through every McCloud in the book until he found the right one. He asked me to have dinner with him, and was extremely polite about it. I told him that I was going to have dinner nearby with my folks that evening and promised that I would come into the store and say hello. My mother and father and I did go in, and he gave them a tour of the place, in the back and all around. Rudy was very charming and they liked him, they were impressed. None of us knew that in the basement was probably the biggest bookie joint in the city of Chicago! I really didn't know anything about that kind of thing in those days. I was just home from my year and a half of college.

After that I went out alone with Rudy for dinner a few times, and he took me around a little bit. We went to the racetrack and I started smoking. I felt like I was growing up, but I was very proper and Rudy acted like a gentleman at all times. He gave me gold cigarette holders and gold cases, which I promptly lost or gave away. I had no sense of the value of things. And Rudy didn't care, he'd just laugh. He seemed to have an endless supply of money, always paying for things with cash, large bills; but he wasn't ostentatious, he had good manners and knew how to have a good time. He was a big drinker but never got drunk. Actually, he was an amazing character and I was fascinated by him. He proposed marriage to me but I was not at all interested; I was just a young girl and wanted to get around, to see the world. I told him, "I haven't seen anything of life yet," and Rudy said, "I'll show you anything you like." He was terrific to know but marriage wasn't what I wanted.

I was going out with several guys then, one of whom was a law student at Northwestern. We'd ride bicycles in Evanston, around the university, and buy ice cream out in No Man's Land along the North shore. He was a nice boy who later became a well-known attorney in Chicago. So I had young friends, too, but I was intrigued by Rudy Winston. I wondered where he got all that money; and I did like the high life, which he knew so well. Whenever I went out of town, like when I returned to Texas, Rudy sent me presents and wrote me little notes; and when I came back to Chicago he was always there, waiting to pick me up at the train station. I was very flattered by this kind of attention. It was hard not to be.

My father was really the one who always wanted to protect me, to see that I didn't have to deal with anything, to worry. He wanted the best for me, to just be a beautiful playgirl. I remember him saying to my mother, "Peggy's a playgirl, a pretty playgirl." And I didn't know what he meant by it. He liked Rudy Winston; he felt that Rudy would take care of me, protect me. Buck liked Rudy, too; or at least he respected him. He knew who he was, that he was involved in the rackets in some way. Rudy was a Jew, the family name had been Weinstein until Rudy's brother had changed it, and that made him seem more exotic to me. And all of the crazy characters he knew! Big guys in immaculate, hand-tailored three piece suits with fancy handkerchiefs sticking out of the breast pocket; weaselly little men in hats who were whispering in Rudy's ear all the time, running in and out. I'd never seen anything like this before. Rudy seemed to be at his store day and night, always willing to take me somewhere, to jump in the big blue Cadillac and take a drive. He offered me a car, or the use of one, the second time we met. What kind of man was this? I wondered. But my family liked him and he certainly was different than anyone I'd ever met before.

After I decided that I didn't want to go back to the University of Texas, where, by the way, I'd won a campus beauty contest—despite my allergies!—which resulted in my being offered a modelling contract by a large agency (I turned it down because I was really in bad shape due to the eczema), I went to New York, to Long Island, to visit my Aunt Maria.

Aunt Maria had a mansion in Hewlett Bay, a big stone house filled with paintings and sculpture and all kinds of would-be actors and actresses, writers and artists, coming and going. She let them use the house as a weekend retreat, fed them, and probably gave most of them money if they needed it. Her own children used to complain about how cheap she was, how she never gave them a dime, instead throwing all of her money away on deadbeat actors and artists. But Aunt Maria did what she wanted; she liked being a part of the art scene, being a benefactress, and she didn't care what her kids thought. I suppose she had a little romance now and then with one of the guys she helped out; I really didn't think much about it at the time, and I don't see why it should have bothered her children the way it apparently did. My mother told me they would complain to her about how Aunt Maria spent her money and about her liaisons. So far as I was concerned, Aunt Maria was a wonderful woman: generous, kind, maybe a bit pretentious in her manner and conversation, but a good soul.

Rudy Winston telephoned me often at Aunt Maria's, and sent

the usual little gifts, so we stayed in contact, but after a while I got very bored staying out in Long Island. I enjoyed listening to the people's stories, about their artistic struggles and difficulties, eating well and being taken care of by Aunt Maria and her staff, but I was feeling restless and decided to move into New York City. The war was on and everything was booming in the city. I loved the bright lights and all of the activity. I got a room in a woman's hotel in midtown Manhattan, The Conroy, I think it was called; it's gone now I later found out that there were some very high-priced call girls working out of that hotel, but I didn't know about it at the time. I was very naive, nineteen years old, and everything fascinated me.

I looked up the modelling agency that had been interested in me after I won the beauty contest at Texas, and started getting some jobs, mostly modelling hats and jewelry. I had some money in my pocket and felt better than I had in a long time. My Aunt Maria was upset, however; I was supposed to be in her care and she feared for my safety in the big city. I had been very protected up to that point and I understood her concern. She called my mother and my brother—who was now a commander in the Navy and living with Laura Mae in Philadelphia—and told them I was too young to be living on my own in Manhattan. She was afraid I'd be led astray. Buck kept in touch; I went down to Philadelphia to visit him and his wife in their beautiful, large apartment near Rittenhouse Square—they had *two* baby grand pianos!—and assured them that I'd be all right, that I was working and not to worry. My brother was busy with his military duties and couldn't spend much time with me and Laura Mae was involved with her society friends, so I went back to New York after a short time.

I dyed my hair black—my long auburn hair—and piled it up on my head, wore some jewelry and only a very little make-up. I succeeded in looking older than I was but retained my legitimate, innocent look. My mother wrote that she was ill and wanted me to come home but I was enjoying myself too much. She was practically bed-ridden by this time because of her worsening heart

36

condition, and I knew that if I went back I'd have to spend my time nursing her. I decided to be a little selfish and stay in New York, telling my father to make sure Rose had enough help around the house. He assured me that he would take care of it; his fur business was going well, he said, and they could afford a full-time maid, so that lessened my guilt feelings. My mother really was more afraid for me than she was feeling sicker; she just wanted her little girl home.

In New York, through my modelling job, I was introduced to many different people, and I started to get around. I had a different date every night and was taken to the best restaurants and night clubs. I learned how to take care of myself. This was in 1943. Men offered to set me up in apartments, to pay all of my bills, and that kind of thing, and I'd just laugh and be nice to them if I felt like it. Then one night I went to a party Harry Cohn, the boss of Columbia Pictures, gave at the Sherry-Netherlands Hotel, or the Warwick, one of those. I couldn't believe how many beautiful young, blonde cuties he had sitting around, all starlets or would-be starlets. It was an amazing party, a great deal of fun, and it was there that I met an exiled White Russian count, Vladimir Kozeny, who became my steady boyfriend.

Kozeny—for some reason I can't recall now I always called him by his last name—had a heart condition, and in his apartment in the Ansonia Hotel on Broadway he had a push-button bed, the kind that was in three sections, because he wasn't supposed to lie down flat. He took me in hand and I thought this was wonderful. The Ansonia was full of mad composers and zany characters who looked like the Marx Brothers. I think Gustav Mahler had once lived there. Kozeny was pals with all of them, they all knew and deferred to him; he was still royalty in that place. Kozeny bought me all kinds of clothes, gorgeous things, only the best. Despite his bad heart we were always on the town—he was proud of me, his young thing, the beautiful model, and he loved showing me off.

Of course all I had to do for Kozeny was go out with him; he really didn't care for more than a little kissing and to put his hand on my leg and have me fuss over him a bit. He wasn't that old, he was in his fifties, and I liked him very much. We'd go to parties and he'd wear a coat with tails and a large red sash across his chest. I didn't realize who most of the people were that I was being introduced to and mixing with: Prince This and Princess That, movie people like Cohn and big-time mobsters. It was the latter that led to my return to Chicago. I didn't know it at the time, but one of those mob guys happened to mention my name to Rudy one day on the phone—I didn't know about Rudy's involvement with these people at this point—and I guess he told my mother or father about it. Anyway, my mother got on the phone and told me that if I didn't come home immediately there was going to be a death in the family. I didn't know if she meant mine or hers but I left New York, and when I got back to Chicago I cried and cried. My mother asked me what was wrong and I said, "I think I'm in love with Kozeny." So my mother got on the phone again and called Kozeny. She told him that if he attempted to contact her daughter he'd be exiled right out of the world. She really did! She went wild and threatened to get Rudy's palookas after him. And this was really the first I heard of Rudy's connections. Of course he was there to welcome me back; he chastised me mildly for running around like I had but Rudy was really very nice and understanding. I'd been in New York for a year or so, I'd had a wonderful fling. I was just twenty and about to begin a totally new phase of my life.

So I was home again. "School or work," said my mother. I didn't want to work, I hated working; modelling was all I knew and I couldn't stand having to smile and be constantly scrutinized like a piece of meat. I'd done that secretarial job for the opera the summer I was sixteen but the idea of doing that again was even worse, and I wasn't really very adept at shorthand and typing. I thought it better to get married. All of my girlfriends were married; but they'd married their high school boyfriends and they were poor, just barely getting along. I didn't want that.

Rudy Winston, of course, was still after me, and I did like him very much. He was very polite and generous and quite an interesting person in his own right. I remember the night he taught me to drive. We came out of the theater and he was suffering from the flu; he'd gotten so sick in the theater that we'd had to leave before the show was over. "Drive the car," he told me, and gave me the keys; he could barely sit up straight in the passenger seat. "I don't have a license," I told him. "I've never even had a lesson!" "Drive it!" he said. It was his new Cadillac— he always had a new Cadillac. So I drove it. We had the wildest ride either of us had ever had. I drove him home and then I drove myself home; he let me keep the car. I went around corners 20,000 miles an hour! And Rudy didn't even bat an eye. He just said, "That's wonderful, Peggy. I thought you told me you'd never driven a car before." He was incredible; he had great faith in me.

He said do this and do that, and here's first gear and here's second. I'd never met anyone like him in my life. He was always so happy with me in those days. He let me do whatever I wanted to. "If you want the car, keep it." he said; and I thought, what a strange man!

Now he began to give me more expensive and glamorous presents. I could go into any store on Michigan Avenue and charge whatever I liked to Rudy. Just sign and take a nice dress, a hat. My mother wanted the good life for me, and she liked Rudy, but he wasn't handsome enough for her. She wanted me to marry a guy like Hal French, a tall, good looking Hal French with money, not a burly, tough guy like Rudy Winston. My father and Rudy got along great; they both liked to drink, and Rudy would take Jack out and they'd have a wonderful time with plenty of booze and showgirls. My father would say, "That Rudy's a swell fellow, you know." And my mother would say, "You don't want to marry him, Peggy. How could you be in the same bathroom with that man? I don't want my beautiful daughter in the same bathroom with a gangster."

My mother got very weird about all of this. She got along all right with Rudy, and didn't hesitate to invoke his name when she threatened poor Vladimir Kozeny on the phone, but marrying him was something else. She knew Rudy had proposed to me several times by now and that I'd developed a mind of my own. Her heart was weak, she couldn't argue as vociferously as she had in the past, and she began to use this argument, based on her health, to try to dissuade me from marrying Rudy. So I was torn between my loyalty to her and the life of luxury Rudy kept promising that I would have if I married him. I truly did not know what to do. My father remained non-committal about the marrying part; he and Rudy were buddies but he left the decision to me.

Rudy went to my mother and said, "Look, Peggy's a nervous wreck. She wants to marry me but she doesn't want to hurt you, she wants to do what you say; she's a good girl. I never had a real mother," he told her, "my mother died before I got to know her, but I'm sure she would have loved Peggy like I do. I'll make Peggy happy, Rose. I'll give her everything she wants and take care of you, too. One thing I'd like from you and Jack, though," he said, "is a big wedding. I'll pay for it, but I want you to put it on. Peggy is the most important thing in the world to me and I want everybody to know about it. I'll be good to her, Rose. Give us your blessing."

My mother said yes, and she and my father paid for the wedding, not Rudy. There must have been five hundred people at the wedding; almost all of them were Rudy's friends and acquaintances, people I'd never seen before. Only about fifty of my friends were there, school girlfriends and their husbands who came in and turned up their noses. Most of them were straight, middle class kids, and Rudy's crowd was a very different league. I looked stunning in an original Lola Soave dress, a long gown, and the kids from my school, my old friends whom I hadn't really seen or been in touch with for some time, didn't quite know what to make of it. I said goodbye to them at my wedding; we were in separate worlds now. Even my own relatives were jealous, surprised. They—except for Aunt Maria, who couldn't come—were just getting by, just starting to make it, and all of a sudden I was already there; it looked like the big time to them and I guess it was. It was a shock to them. The party was held at the Blackstone Hotel. The mayor was there, we received a wire from the governor wishing us well, and I remember my mother whispering to my father, "Jack, who was that nice man I was just speaking with?" "Al Capone's brother," he told her. I believe Al Capone was in Alcatraz by this time.

Rudy and I went to Lake Placid, New York, for our honeymoon. We walked in the woods and went swimming—though Rudy couldn't swim, he never did learn how. There were all kinds of things Rudy couldn't do but tried for my sake. He'd never bowled before, and I loved to bowl, so he'd just pick up a ball and, in his own unorthodox fashion, roll the ball down the alley a hundred miles an hour—he had tremendous strength—and knock all the pins down! He said he was the best dancer in the world, but he didn't know how to dance at all. We got out on the dance floor and he danced every dance. He was a riot! He did everything even if he couldn't do it. Rudy had no fear of anything, and he had a great sense of humor to go along with an outrageous temper. He never showed the temper to me but I'd heard stories about him from his friends. Rudy did some business in New York while we were there, in the city. I went shopping and he saw whomever he had to, he never discussed it with me. We went out on the town with two sons of the owner of a large theater chain; they were with their girlfriends, not their wives, and afterwards Rudy told me he wouldn't run around on me like that. To tell the truth the thought hadn't crossed my mind; I was used to the behavior of my father and brother and I hadn't intended to make Rudy promise me anything. I was glad to be married but I hadn't really considered what that meant.

When Rudy and I came home from our honeymoon I wanted to get an apartment or a house but Rudy said no, we had to live near his store, near Rush Street, so we rented a suite in the Seneca Hotel on Chestnut Street. I knew the Castle boys, who owned the drugstore in the Palmer House, where we used to go often for dinner, and they offered me a job selling perfume; they wanted me to talk to customers about their line of fine French perfumes. This was to be a part-time job, more or less at my own convenience, but Rudy said no, I couldn't work, not his wife; he would give me an allowance of twenty-five dollars a week. I could go into any store and charge whatever I wanted; I could eat in the finest restaurants and never be presented with a bill; I could have my own Cadillac or any other car I wanted; but I wasn't allowed to have any cash in my hand other than the twenty-five dollars Rudy gave me each week. He was the boss.

It was a fast crowd that stayed at the Seneca in those days. Most of the guests lived there on a permanent basis or else kept a room for whenever they might need it. Eddie Danillo, who owned the Milwaukee Ace brewery, lived next door to us. Eddie was a nice guy. I knew he was connected with the Mafia, but I didn't think that was a big deal; everybody I met with Rudy had shady dealings. Danillo owned a couple of clothing stores, too, and one day he knocked on our door and gave me a box with a big ribbon on it. He said, "This is for you. I hope you like it," and then he

43

left. There was a very nice hat in the box, from one of his stores. I liked the hat and wore it that night to dinner.

We were just leaving the restaurant when who should come in but Eddie Danillo. "Gee, that hat looks great on you," he said to me. I thanked him and said to Rudy, "Yes, Eddie gave me this hat today. Wasn't that nice of him?" "Eddie gave you that hat?" Rudy said. "Yes, why?" I asked. "Wait outside for me, Peggy," Rudy told me. "I'll be right there." I went outside and the next thing I knew there was a loud crash from inside the restaurant. I ran back in and there was Eddie Danillo on the floor with pieces of glass all over him: Rudy had knocked him down through a plate glass window in the foyer. Rudy was calm and smiling. The maitre d' was saying to him, "It's all right, Mr. Winston, we'll take care of everything, there's no problem, no problem." Rudy and I left and I said, "You're crazy. Why did you knock Eddie down? Because he gave me a hat?" Rudy stopped and looked at me; he wasn't smiling. "I knocked him down because he didn't *ask me* first if it was all right to give you the hat." "But he's in the Mafia, isn't he?" I said. "You can't go around beating up guys in the Mafia!" Rudy just laughed. "You know," he said, "that hat really does look good on you." The next day or maybe the day after there was an item in one of the newspaper gossip columns about Rudy knocking somebody through a plate glass window, but Eddie's name wasn't mentioned. After that Eddie and I always smiled and said hello to one another whenever we met, but he never gave me any more presents.

I became immersed in Rudy's world. Most of his so-called friends I had no use for. One of his closest buddies was a detective from the local precinct named Bill Moore. What a rotten guy he was. Every once in a while he'd use me to identify a suspect for some crime or another. Of course I'd never seen the guy before in my life. "He's no good, Peggy," Bill would say, "that's the guy who did it." And I'd have to say yes, I was there at the scene, I saw it on the street, I was passing by. Oh, it was horrible. I did it because Rudy said go on, help Bill out, he's a pal. I refused to ever testify at any trials but that didn't matter, they never asked me to do that, only to identify someone in a lineup. Who knows who they were or what they'd really done, if anything, or what happened to them?

Every now and then I'd be coming to the pharmacy when Rudy didn't expect me and there would be some policemen carting him off to jail. He'd shout, "Don't worry, Peggy, I'll be back in an hour!" And he would be. This was because of the book they were running in the basement. Rudy would have to make large "donations" to the Policemen's Benevolent Association so that he wouldn't get busted too often. "Why not?" he'd joke, "I'm a benevolent guy."

Rush Street was glorious in those days: the nightclubs were flourishing, business was good; it was a twenty-four hour part of town. It was exciting, but I was picking up the wrong values. My mother didn't like it, didn't like the life I was leading. There was a great deal of drinking and we went out every night for dinner, which I did not want; I loved to cook, I was a good cook, my mother had taught me, and I begged Rudy to let me make him dinner at home. But then he'd show up with some stranger, some drunk, and I wouldn't let him in the house. "But this guy is a celebrity," Rudy would say. I'd get angry and slam the door on them. "I don't care who it is," I'd yell, "he's dead drunk. I don't want him in here!"

There were some nice people, though, like Barney Ross, the former boxing champion. Barney used to come into the suite at the Seneca and play the piano and tell me his life story, which was pathetic. He'd become a junkie while he was in the military hospital recovering from his war wounds. Barney was on and off the hop when I knew him; I never knew if the light was on or off, as we used to say, but he was a sweetheart. A lot of boys, of course, like Eddie Danillo, were mob guys—we never mentioned the word Mafia unless we were alone—but then there were others. Dick Bagdasarian, an Armenian who'd made a fortune as a bootlegger in the twenties, lived across the hall from us. He and his wife

45

would go out and give their dog, a poodle, to their chauffeur and tell him to walk it. Bobby, the chauffeur, would drive the dog over to Rudy's store, put it up on the counter and have a cup of coffee. Years later my son Jimmy would sit at that counter and dunk doughnuts in the coffee and feed it to the organ grinder's pet monkey and the Bagdasarians' poodle. Another neighbor was Buddy Harvey, who was married to one of Tommy Manville's ex-wives—the eighth, I think—and I loved her. Sunny Ainsworth was her name, she was okay in my book.

One time my mother came to visit and she went to the hairdresser in the building. I came walking in and the hairdresser or the manicurist said, "Look at that young punk, with that $10,000 mink coat. Who does she think she is anyway?" And my mother said, "That's my daughter." My folks would come and have Sunday dinner with us, but my mother was becoming increasingly disturbed by my life, and so was I.

Then I got pregnant. I remember wearing my little pea jacket and blue beret and going to the gynecologist with my mother; Dr. Marshall, who was the finest gynecologist in Chicago, a wonderful man, who's gone now. Dr. Marshall confirmed it and I was thrilled that I was going to have a child, but my mother was heartbroken. "You're too young," she told me. "No, I'm not," I said. "I've been married over a year. This is great. I want a nice little girl to keep me company. I'm alone so often at night."

I really wanted my own house or apartment, I disliked living in a hotel. I knew Rudy liked it, but I wanted a place that I could furnish myself, to have my own things, my own furniture. I wanted to be able to clean my own house, not have a hotel maid. Rudy loved the fast life, living it up; he'd consume at least a bottle of sparkling burgundy or champagne with dinner every night, even on those rare occasions he'd allow me to cook a meal for him alone. There was so much heavy drinking around me! Rudy could drink two bottles of wine with dinner and then go on drinking Irish whiskey all night, until four or five in the morning and he'd never be drunk. Other people would fall out, collapse, but not

46

Rudy. He was a prodigious drinker and the amazing thing was that he always kept his wits; he never lost control of the situation.

We lived on the sixteenth floor and one night while I was lying in bed, thinking about my life, a bird flew in the open window. I was really petrified by this bird that was madly careening around the room, going around and around. This was after I was pregnant, I already had a big stomach. I called down to the desk and asked them for help, to get the bird out. They thought I was out of my mind, or that I'd been drinking. I said no, there's a bird going wild in here and I'm not drinking or anything. The bird was batting itself against the walls and splattering blood all over the place. And I thought, this is a bad sign; I'd never been superstitious before, but I couldn't help having this thought. This is no good, I thought, what does it mean? Finally a bellhop came up and knocked on the door. He came in and looked at me; the bird had stopped knocking into walls and was cowering on the floor in a corner. I showed the bellboy where it was and then he knew I wasn't crazy, and he took it out.

The bird was the first "sign" I had that I recognized. Many years later, the night after my mother's funeral, I was sitting in my bedroom in the house on Rockwell Street with my son Jimmy when a giant golden moth appeared at the window and began banging itself against the glass. It was the middle of the winter and there were no moths that I knew of, especially large golden ones like that, flying around outside at that time of year. My first thought was that it was the spirit of my mother, it was Rose coming back to see me. The moth frightened me even more than the bird had, and I remember turning off the light and waiting in the dark, hugging Jimmy, for a half hour or so. When I turned the light on again the moth was gone, but I couldn't shake the conviction that it had been a manifestation of my mother.

Rudy's older brother Bruno owned a couple of automobile agencies and a piece of the Chez Paree night club. Bruno sort of ruled Rudy, he was a tough guy, too, and Rudy looked up to him; he listened to what Bruno told him. Bruno and I got along well

47

enough; he was much older than I was, in his forties, and we never really had too much to do with one another. Rudy and Bruno and I were at a ringside table at the Chez Paree watching Sophie Tucker when I went into labor. I almost had my baby right there on the table in the Chez Paree, but Rudy rushed me out and around to Passavant Hospital where I had my son, Jimmy—James Barry Winston, named after a brother of my father's who had died young. So I had a little boy now, not the girl I'd been certain I was going to have, and I was very happy.

Rudy was overjoyed to have a son, the first boy in the family to be born in America. Rudy had come with his family to Chicago from Austria when he was seven years old, and Bruno had yet to have children. It was a great moment for Rudy, he was so proud. Jimmy's birth was the lead item in the *Tribune* gossip column the next morning, "Talk of the Town." My hospital room was filled with flowers, all from "the boys." They overflowed into the hall and I told the nurses to please give them to the other patients who might like to have them. Everything was fine, but I couldn't get the thought of the bird out of my mind. I knew it had been a sign, but I wasn't sure of what.

Buck seemed to be very proud of his wife when he married her. Laura Mae Allen had university degrees both in French and mathematics and had taught both on the college level. Not only was she very bright but also glamorous; she had a marvelous figure, platinum blonde hair that was completely natural and a sharp tongue. She was also extremely avaricious, acquisitive and narrow-minded; she was anti-Semitic, anti-Catholic and anti-people of any color other than white. She came from a staunch Republican family that was part Scotch-English and part French. To the Allen family, there was no religion other than Episcopalian.

When I spent the summer with her and Buck in South Carolina, she instructed me that I was not to speak with any man other than an officer. When I'd come upon a nice young boy who wanted to take me out, who was not an officer, Laura Mae would say, "Don't talk to him, Peggy, he's beneath us." She presided over the dinner table like the great lady she thought she was but was not. Laura Mae thought it was just horrible that I had gone to Catholic school. I'm not sure how she dealt with the fact that Buck had been raised in a Catholic household; she certainly didn't get along very well with my parents.

However, Laura Mae took a great liking to me, and despite all of her horrible traits I managed to get along with her. She took me under her wing and sought to instruct me in what she thought was the proper manner to behave, what to like and not to like, whom to associate with, and so on.

49

One time Buck and I were preparing to go sailing and Laura Mae came down to the dock and said, "You can go sailing for a couple of hours, but don't forget that we have guests arriving at five o'clock. Make sure you're back in time to be dressed for dinner." Well, Buck and I didn't get back until after midnight. We sailed off in Buck's little ketch, wearing only our bathing suits, on what was at that point a nice warm day. A storm sprang up while we were out on the ocean and we lost control of the boat. I was scared to death as all of these mountainous waves came over us, almost swamping the boat. Buck kept shouting, "Bail, Peggy, bail!" I found a tin can and did what I could. In the middle of the worst part of it I suddenly found that I wasn't scared anymore. I laughed and yelled, "Davey Jones's locker here we come!" Buck thought I was crazy.

We went through some rigorous maneuvers out there and finally drifted to an island; but we couldn't get off the boat because the shale was so sharp that it would cut our feet. Somehow Buck re-rigged the sail and we managed to get home. Laura Mae was furious, of course, but then she saw how shaken both Buck and I were and was good to me, and helped me to bed. I had nightmares every night for a week after that, thinking that the bed was moving. I woke up screaming more than once; the window curtains were flying into the room with the breeze and I imagined they were big waves coming at me, or a big shark. It was horrible.

When I married Rudy, Laura Mae refused to attend the wedding. She made some excuse about having to stay in Philadelphia but I knew that she looked down her nose at Rudy and his people. My mother thought it no great loss that Laura Mae wasn't there; at least Buck was, and after that Laura Mae and I weren't so close. She had started drinking heavily by this time, anyway, and was already something of an alcoholic. I knew that my mother was disappointed in both Buck's and my marriages, but there really was nothing to do about it; I did feel guilty about not being able to please her. I soon learned that it was going to be even more difficult for me to be able to please myself.

Six months after Jimmy was born Rudy and I took a trip to the West Coast, stopping in Las Vegas on the way. We left Jimmy with his nursemaid, Flo, at my parents' house, and flew out to Vegas. Rudy had some business there. He was pals with Ben Siegel, known in the press as "Bugsy"—he *hated* that nickname and I never heard anyone call him that to his face—and Ben had told us to stay in his suite at the Flamingo.

Ben, originally from New York, where he'd been a cohort of Meyer Lansky's, had established Las Vegas as a gambling mecca for the Chicago mob. He came into Rudy's store whenever he was in town, and sent me the largest bouquet of flowers I received when Jimmy was born.

We had a great time in Vegas—Ben wasn't in town, he was in Los Angeles—and Rudy did whatever business he had to while I gambled a little and stayed by the pool. Las Vegas was still in its infancy then, and everything was very new and exciting and seemingly innocent. All of the Chicago boys were there, so it was like old home week only we were at an oasis in the desert. Everything was first class, Rudy and I were treated with the utmost deference and I felt wonderful being on the go again.

We spent a couple of weeks in Las Vegas and then drove a rented car to Los Angeles. When we got there we checked into the old Ambassador Hotel and Rudy called Eddie Hill, Ben's girlfriend Virginia's brother, to say hello. Ginny Hill didn't like Vegas, and spent most of her time in L.A. and Paris. I had met her several times in Chicago, where we'd gone shopping together on Michigan Avenue. Like Laura Mae, Ginny felt protective of me and liked to have me along. I was young and innocent and I suppose these older, more sophisticated women enjoyed showing me the ropes. Anyhow, as it turned out, while we had been travelling to Los Angeles from Las Vegas, Ben Siegel had been shot dead in Virginia Hill's house.

Ginny was in Europe, and Eddie said to lie low; nobody knew what might happen next. Rudy told me not to worry, that everything was all right, but I got very scared all of a sudden. I began to appreciate the reality of the situation, to really consider for the first time just who it was I had been hanging around with and what my husband did for a living. Until this point I'd been on a kind of cloud, just going along thinking that soon I'd have my little house, a nice family of my own, a husband who came home for dinner every night; a normal life. Now I saw what was going on, and I didn't want it.

Fortunately Rudy was out of the hotel room when Eddie Hill called back. "Hi, Peg," he said. "You know things are in a bit of an upheaval right now, and Virginia's out of town, but is there anything I can do for you? Can I get you a car? Take you someplace?" I just said, "Thank you so much, Ed. If we want anything we'll let you know. We have everything we need, thank you." And I never told Rudy about Eddie Hill's call; in fact, I told him that Ed had never called. I didn't want anything to do with that bunch anymore.

We stayed in L.A. for a few days. We went sightseeing and did the usual touristy things. Rudy steered clear of "business" and we had a lovely time. My father's old friend Don Gilbert, an associate from his days in the millinery business, was living there and Rudy and I looked him up. Don had married a much younger woman, also named Peggy, and we got along wonderfully. Of course they knew their way around so we put them in the back seat of our Caddy covertible and away we went, touring along the coast of

California. We really had a delightful time with the Gilberts. We drove up to San Francisco and then to Reno, where Rudy received a message telling him to return to Las Vegas, which we did. Back in Vegas Rudy went off with the guys while I hung out at the pool, like before; but this time the heat began to get to me, I was uncomfortable, and I was nervous about this mob business. If they'd killed Ben Siegel they could certainly kill Rudy or anybody else. I tried to talk to Rudy about it but he said everything was fine, nothing more was going to happen, that's the way it went sometimes. Apparently Ben had overreached himself in Vegas in some way and hadn't been able to work it out. The only mention I heard made of Ben's murder was one night at dinner in Vegas when a man I'd never met before, someone in the warehouse business from Cleveland, I think, said, "It's Lansky, they wouldn't have done it without him." Rudy seemed to be in good spirits again, and that was the end of it.

I met Larry Adler, the harmonica player, in Vegas, and we became very friendly. He was a smart young man, a sweet, lovely guy; a very slight fellow, he looked as if a small breeze could blow him over. We'd sit around talking, I don't know what about. I don't even know if I had anything to say in those days. I was the playgirl, like my father had said, I looked nice all the time. It wasn't too long after this—during the McCarthy era—that poor Larry Adler was forced to leave the country, accused of being a Communist. I don't know anything about that, but he was a gentleman, a fine person, as well as a marvelous musician.

I also met some divorce lawyers from Chicago in Las Vegas. One of them was treating his girlfriend of the moment so horribly that I said to her, "How can you stand him?" I didn't know then that later on this man would represent me in my divorce from Rudy.

53

When we returned to Chicago I found that my mother's health had deteriorated. It was decided that she should spend the winter months in a warm climate so Rudy told me to take Rose and Jimmy down to Florida, where I rented a house in Miami Beach. We wound up taking a long term lease on the house, and kept it for several years. I loved Miami; the sunshine was good for my skin and I didn't have many outbreaks of eczema. Jimmy ran around with nothing but his shorts or swimming trunks on and my mother was able to rest and sit in the sun.

Rudy would come down for weekends and we'd usually take off for Cuba. I was, naturally, never one to be alone without a gentleman around. Not that I was doing anything wrong, but when I was alone I always had a dinner date and so forth. I'd meet interesting people, and when Rudy came down I'd be able to introduce him to them. One fellow offered us the use of his apartment in Havana, and we went over and stayed there for a while; then Rudy and I rented a house on Verodero Beach, which I thought was the most beautiful place I'd ever seen. We had a nice little place on the edge of the DuPont estate, which was being constructed at the time. The tradewinds blew constantly and we didn't need screens on the windows because there weren't any mosquitoes or flies. A husband and wife cooked our food and took care of the house and it was heaven. Cuba was a paradise for rich

Americans in those days. In later years, just after Castro had taken over, my father went to Havana with Buck, who was smuggling money out of the country for refugees, and he loved to stand on the corners of the main streets downtown and watch the sexy Cuban women walk by without girdles. That was my father in his old age. Cuba's changed, of course, since then. Those were nice years, nice trips. Rudy had his dealings with the boys in Havana—Lansky's headquarters, as I remember, were in the Hotel Nacional—but so long as I had my place on Verodero Beach nothing bothered me.

Back in Chicago, however, I began to have serious trouble with Rudy. I was tired of the bums he hung out with and his always having to be at the store. If I had been able to have my own house and not had to live in the hotel things would have been better, but Rudy wouldn't allow it. The glamor of chasing around to different nightclubs and restaurants paled. Rudy was always at the store, treating some showgirl for a boil or a pimple, taking them in the back, girls with nothing on under their mink coats, and giving them a shot of penicillin for the clap or a bad cold. Rudy would take care of everything, everyone loved him around there. He was a marvelous pharmacist and a forceful salesman. Rudy could sell you something white when you wanted black. He was amazing that way. If he could take advantage of someone businesswise, he didn't lose a moment; outside of business though, he'd give you the shirt off his back.

Aside from the drugstore Rudy had a variety of businesses: car agencies with Bruno, interest in a couple of restaurants, a wholesale liquor warehouse. We never had a bank account; Rudy kept his money in safety deposit boxes in the big hotels. Whenever he needed to make a "deposit" he'd have me go over with the cash and put it in the box. There was a different safety deposit box for every dealing: one for the racing book at the Drake, one for the liquor store at the Ambassador, and so on. The money meant nothing to me, I never saw it; I just put it in the vaults. Sometimes

55

Rudy would give me too much cash and I'd have to bring it back to him. "Why didn't you put it in the box?" he'd say, and I'd tell him that I couldn't stuff any more in, it was too full.

I finally convinced Rudy to invest some money in a building on the near North side, an apartment house. It was a grand old building with gorgeous flats, and I said, "How long before one of these apartments will be vacant? How long before we can move in?" I was tired of life in the Seneca; it was no place to raise a family, Jimmy was getting older. I didn't like being used by my friends in the hotel who would say to me, "Don't tell Frank that I was out drinking this afternoon with Ralph, okay honey? Tell him I was with you." That kind of stuff.

Of course it was interesting when someone like Ginger Rogers or Tony Martin came into town. They were friends of Rudy's and I liked to go over to wherever they were staying and have dinner and talk. Ginger Rogers's mother was always entertaining for Rudy, she loved him; and Rudy would say to everyone, "Oh you have to meet my beautiful wife." I must admit he was constant, he did love me. I wondered whether or not I really loved him, though. It was the glamor, the high life that I'd been attracted to, but it was now wearing thin.

Rudy had an aunt, Jennie Ashkenaz, who was like a mother to him. Jennie and her husband, Lou, were very well off. Lou had made his money in the beer business, and in their old age their great passion was the racetrack. Jennie used to love to take me with her out to Sportsman's or Arlington or Maywood, wherever the horses were running. She taught me to always look down on the ground at the track in case somebody had dropped some money or a good ticket, and she taught me how to read the *Racing Form*. Jennie was in her sixties then, a tiny, bird-like woman with dyed black hair and a little rosebud mouth full of lipstick. I loved her, we thought alike, and she showed me how to make Jewish dishes. We'd prepare big dinners together for Lou and Rudy in her magnificent Lake Shore Drive apartment that was filled with fine antiques. One time Rudy called up and said he couldn't make it for dinner, he was tied up at the store. I was about to say all right and hang up but Jennie took the phone and yelled at him, telling Rudy to get there as soon as possible if he knew what was good for him. And he came right over! She was full of the devil and a great friend; there wasn't anything anyone could put over on Lou or Jennie.

Jennie made sure that her daughters, all four of them, married millionaires. Her daughter Gloria's husband went to prison for his father, and when he got out he collected a few million bucks. This was before I knew Rudy. Gloria was in love with Rudy and while her husband was in jail they had some kind of affair; they were first cousins. Gloria was beautiful but nutty, and after her husband got out they resumed the marriage. Jennie knew about Gloria's crush on Rudy, in fact she was the one who told me about it, but she never let on to Rudy that she knew, and I never mentioned it to him.

When I married Rudy, Rachel, Jennie and Lou's oldest daughter, who had married into high society in Chicago, threw a dinner party for us. Rudy's family, with the exception of his sister, Irma, were all wonderful to me, they wanted to show me off. I was still modelling a little then and of course Rudy always saw to it that I had the most beautiful clothes and hats. I tried my best to get along with Irma, too, but she was very cold and made me feel like I was stealing her brother away from her. Jennie didn't much care for Irma and when Rachel didn't invite her to the dinner party she had for Rudy and me Irma held it against me, and we never did become friends.

Jennie was a good friend, but I was lonely. A fellow named Bob Rawson came to dinner one night with us and the next day he came over to the hotel to see me. He was a gorgeous man, an Army major at the time, and he wanted to have an affair with me. I felt like running away with him. He was so handsome that I was tempted, I was just momentarily stricken. I turned him down, I wouldn't sleep with him. And I didn't hide it from Rudy. I told him how lonely I was, how I wanted to move, how tempted I'd been to go off with Bob Rawson. Rudy got angry, of course, and said, "If he comes near here I'll beat him up." Rudy was half Bob Rawson's size but I knew he meant it and I made sure I never saw Rawson again. I had so many opportunities like that, but I didn't like the crowd we were running around with; they were all phonies and hot shots with a lot of money and no sense.

Everything felt wrong to me. I felt that I'd rather be on a tropical island with only my bathing suit, drinking coconut milk and watching my son play in the sand. I wanted to take Jimmy and run away for good. My eczema came back, I started going to different doctors, and finally I had it over my entire body, including my face, where I'd never had it before. I was a mess.

Rudy liked to live hard, to be on the go every minute of the day. He had tremendous energy and had more friends than anyone I've ever known. There's a plaque up in Holy Name Cathedral in Chicago with his name on it, which is a great honor. The Bishop used to call Rudy up when he was sick and have him come over to talk with him and show him how to take his medicine. We were friends with the owners of the Club Alabam, a place for all of the visiting firemen and cheating husbands. The club had pretty good food, good entertainment, and the showgirls made a lot of money on the side. We used to go riding at the stables the Alabam owners kept in the country. Rudy was pals with Tony Zale, the boxer, who had a restaurant across the street. One night I walked over to the store and there were Rudy and Tony standing in the street, watching a fellow sweep up broken glass from the sidewalk. I asked what had happened and Tony laughed. "Rudy put another guy through the window," he said. I remembered Eddie Danillo, and asked Rudy why he'd done it. "The guy was giving one of the girls a hard time," Rudy said, meaning one of the showgirls from next door. "She was having a cup of coffee and he wouldn't leave her alone, so I threw him out." "Yeah, only he forgot to open the door first," said Tony.

This kind of thing went on all the time. I was fed up with all of Rudy's hoodlum friends, the so-called celebrities and tough-guy talk. It appealed to me after a drink or two, when I would enjoy the atmosphere; but the next morning I was always sorry to have been a part of it, to have allowed these people over to mess up the place. Rudy liked to have people around and have parties, and there was no limit to the booze. He brought up one case of sparkling burgundy after another, that and whatever else anyone wanted.

After a particularly wild party that had lasted into the wee hours of the morning, after all of the people had gone, I looked around at the debris and then at Rudy, who was saying, "Come on, Peg, let's have one more drink." I looked straight at him and said,

"You know, I'm going to leave you. I want a divorce." I told him that I was serious, I didn't like this life. Rudy turned pale and said if I left him he would commit suicide. "I'm going to get outside and walk around the sixteenth floor on the side of the building," he said. "If you don't stay with me I'll jump off." It was the alcohol talking, of course, and he didn't go out the window. He cried and put his head in my lap, so I said all right, but that we had to try to make a stab at more down to earth living. Rudy cried and cried and said yes, he'd slow down, things would be different, Jimmy and I were all he had. I didn't believe him but he was my husband and I couldn't leave; not yet, anyway.

Soon after this my eczema worsened and infection set in. I told Rudy I had to get away and took Jimmy to my mother's house. I was hospitalized because I was running a fever and my skin was blistered from head to toe. The doctors called it neurodermatitis and I was swathed in bandages. My skin would stick to the bandages and when they were unwound I'd scream. The doctors admitted they didn't know what to do with me, they were experimenting.

I was given an oil bath every day, in order to loosen the bandages, and put under a heat lamp. Medical students were brought in to see me, the worst case of dermatitis they'd ever had. I looked like The Mummy. Rudy's brother Bruno didn't believe that I was as sick as I was; he told Rudy he thought I was faking, I was acting, it couldn't be that bad. Rudy brought him to the hospital and he was horrified; I smelled so badly from the open sores that Bruno couldn't take it, he had to leave.

I was in a private room, and Rudy made sure that I was given the best care. I remember during this time thinking that perhaps I never would get better, that I'd always have to be wrapped up, hidden. One of my favorite films from around that time was *Pepe Le Moko*, with Jean Gabin starring as a Parisian gangster hiding out in Algiers, and I imagined myself living the rest of my life covered up like an Arab woman, sequestered in the Kasbah.

After two months in the hospital my condition began to

improve. My face cleared up first and one day the doctor walked in and said, "My, what a pretty young girl." He'd never been able to see my face before. Amazingly, I didn't have a scar. The doctors suggested to Rudy that he take me away on a long trip, take me someplace where I wouldn't have any aggravation and could recover my health. So Rudy made arrangements for Jimmy to stay at my parents' house and we left for Hawaii.

Rudy thought that he could do some business in the islands—I guess the boys were opening up some operations out there—and I was just glad to get out of the hospital. A girlfriend of mine, Arlene Carrol, who'd been a high fashion model in Chicago and New York, and had been a *Vanity Fair* cover girl, had married a doctor from Honolulu and with him had opened up one of the swankiest resort hotels in Hawaii. Rudy and I rented one of their cottages and Arlene saw to it that I had everything I needed. It must have been very expensive but Rudy didn't care. Nothing was too good for his wife.

I spent six months in Hawaii, living in a bathing suit with no make-up, only an orchid in my hair. Rudy was back and forth between Honolulu and Chicago, and through his business associates and Arlene Carrol we met some wonderful people, most of whom were Chinese. We went to the Chinese theater, and to the Kabuki, marvelous outdoor restaurants, and had the best time of our lives. Rudy made a few very successful contacts and established a racing book and gambling casino, so he was happy. I regained my health and felt and looked like a million dollars.

As soon as we got back to Chicago, however, I began to get nervous again. The same old lifestyle resumed and I knew that if I didn't make a change I'd break down in the same way, only worse. This time when I told Rudy I was leaving he didn't argue with me. He was very unhappy about it but said all right, let's try it living apart for a while. We decided to separate, not divorce immediately, and see what happened. I went to my mother's with Jimmy; she was glad to have me living at home, and I went out with Rudy at night.

Jennie Ashkenaz begged me to give Rudy another chance; she desperately wanted to keep me in the family. She promised that I would have money, jewelry, whatever I wanted, but I couldn't do it, I rebelled. I didn't want to be the "playgirl" anymore, the pretty girl always on display. I didn't have anything of my own, not really. I was continually put down by Rudy and he was incapable of understanding how I felt. He loved me, that was true, he promised me the moon, but he couldn't see the problem. My mother kept after me to divorce Rudy, to make another, cleaner life for myself; so I did, I got a divorce. Rudy bought off my attorney—the guy I'd met in Las Vegas a couple of years or so before—and I was awarded twenty-five dollars a week for Jimmy, that's all. Rudy paid for the attorney.

I didn't care about not getting a large settlement, I was free. I thought to myself, now my troubles are over; but they were only just beginning.

My mother was too sick to look after Jimmy all of the time, and I couldn't afford to have Flo or another girl around, so I stayed home. It was difficult, though, because I didn't want to place the entire financial burden on my father. Through an old girlfriend of my brother's I got a job working at the Furniture Mart on Fridays. I was called a Friday Girl and showed customers the line and made cocktails at four o'clock. It was very easy, all I had to do was look nice and be sharp with the customers, the buyers, be able to talk intelligently and keep them happy. It wasn't much of a job but I did make a little money and contacts with the various wholesalers in case I wanted anything at cost.

The buyers would bring me presents, silk stockings, flowers, boxes of chocolates, and ask me out; but I didn't want to date. The other girls would say that I was being silly, that I should take advantage of the situation and begin dating again. I had had it with the high life, I didn't want it anymore. I didn't want to run out and smoke and drink. In fact, I had given up smoking, mainly because I lost too many gold cigarette cases and I thought it was a waste of money. Rudy and I would go into El Morocco and I'd leave the case on the table. I'd want to go back to get it but he'd just say, "Leave it, don't worry. I'll buy you another one." Rudy was crazy that way, he had a strange attitude about things, especially where I was concerned. He wanted complete control over me and I was loath to become involved with another man who might try to do the same thing.

After a while, after more prodding by the girls at work and encouragement from my mother, I began to go out on dates. I made great demands of my suitors, however. I expected them to bring me gifts of the finest French perfume on the first date, to come to the door with flowers for my mother. This is what I had learned to expect, and if they didn't do it I didn't have to go out with them. I really was longing for a nice boy, to have a little house of my own, more children; this is how I felt. But men were always putting me in a different role: they would take me out and buy me beautiful things and put me on a pedestal, the beautiful princess. I wanted these nice things, I was used to them, but at the same time I wanted to settle down in a modest way. I was confused, mixed up; I knew and I didn't know. To what standards should I conform? I was secretly battling with my desire to call my old boyfriend Hal French, but my ego, my pride, wouldn't permit me to do it. I don't know that Hal would have been the answer to my confusion but I never allowed myself to find out.

I'd drive by the middle and upper middle class homes with lights on in the windows and I'd picture the mother in the kitchen, the father sitting in the living room reading his paper and smoking his pipe—like a frame from a Frank Capra film, *It's A Wonderful Life*—that kind of sentimental, homey scene. It frustrated me to think about it, because Rudy and I had certainly had the money to live that way, and I couldn't have it. I was very upset about this for a very long time, and I blamed Rudy, rightly or wrongly, for preventing me from establishing this kind of idealized lifestyle.

My mother was doing what she could with Jimmy but she began, finally, to throw up to me the fact that I left him with her so much. She didn't feel it was good for her health, that it was putting an undue hardship on her. She was right, I knew this, and I felt guilty about it. Years later I felt that I had unnecessarily contributed to the premature death of my mother, that I had given her too much work to do, had burdened her with the care of my son.

When Rudy and I had gotten divorced the photographers had come to the court and, foolishly, I'd let them take my picture while I was sitting on the top of a desk with my legs crossed. The next day in the newspaper they blew the case out of proportion, running a photo of me with a big smile and my skirt hiked up under the headline, "Chicago Debutante Divorces Playboy." The story said that Rudy had one hundred suits and two hundred ties in his closet, quoting him to the effect that he'd rather live in the closet than with me, that kind of nonsense. I didn't think much about it at the time, I laughed it off, but for months afterward I received crank calls. This, too, upset my mother.

Not long after the divorce my mother and I were sitting and talking and she reminded me of an incident that occurred when I was seventeen years old. She and I had been walking downtown in the Loop, the streets were very crowded, and a man came up to us holding a camera. He asked my mother, while he was looking at me, if he could take my picture. He said there was a contest where Dorothy Lamour was going to choose a girl to have a screen test, and the contest photographers were stopping girls on the street, wherever they spotted an attractive young lady, and photographing them. The finalists were to be invited to the Chicago theater on State Street for the judging. We allowed him to go ahead and take my picture and a few days later I received a call asking me to come down to the theater. There was a group photo taken in the lobby of the theater, which I was in, but then I got so shy that I made some excuse about having to go to the restroom and instead of going up on stage with the other girls, I ran out the door.

"You were such a good girl, Peggy," said my mother as she recalled the incident. "You were so shy and afraid to offend anyone. I thought everything would be so wonderful for you, so easy." I knew she was disappointed with what I'd done with my life so far, and I was determined to change direction. I just wasn't sure how to go about it.

A holiday Rudy and I spent in Jamaica had a bearing on my future. Neither of us had ever been there before, and we went to a new resort called Tower Isle in Ochos Rios. I was sitting around the first day in Ochos Rios when a photographer came up and asked if I would be the model on the cover of their new travel brochures. It was great fun, I posed along with several other models, and Rudy and I met a number of interesting people. Foremost among them, as far as I was concerned, was Johnny Reata, whose family owned many different businesses in Kingston and other places throughout the Caribbean. Johnny had been born in Venezuela and was extremely handsome, with wavy black hair and a red mustache—his mother's grandfather, he said, had had red hair. Johnny took us all over the island and showed us a wonderful time.

Johnny was a friend of Errol Flynn's, whose yacht, the *Zaca*, was anchored in the harbor when we were there. Flynn was a real dare-devil, Johnny told us. He would dive off his boat in the middle of the open sea and take a swim, making sure that his henchman stood guard with a high-powered rifle in case a shark came along. Flynn would swim ashore from his anchorage, which was quite a ways out, but, as Johnny would say, that was Flynn. One afternoon Johnny and Rudy and I were sitting around the pool when Flynn came over, followed by his bodyguards, to say hello to Johnny. We were introduced and Flynn, who really was a handsome man, took my hand and kissed it, but as he did he just kept on going and fell down right on the ground in front of me—he was intoxicated! I met him again later and he was charming but nervous, probably because he was drinking so heavily all the time.

Johnny Reata knew everyone in Jamaica, he was a splendid host, and after Rudy and I left, he kept in touch. When he heard that Rudy and I had divorced, Johnny flew to Chicago—he had business there, he said—and took me out to dinner. The next day he went to my father and asked for my hand in marriage.

The Reata family were strict Catholics, and they were all very wealthy. Johnny's older brother married a girl from the Bronx and was in the shipbuilding business. Their father, the old man, drove around in a big car with a chauffeur trying to pick up pretty girls. It was quite a family. There had been a great deal of intermarriage within the family, cousin marrying cousin, and as a result many of the children turned out to be deaf or mute or blind from birth. Arturo, the older brother, really oversaw the family, he took care of everything. Johnny had been married once, was separated, and kept his children in a Catholic school in Caracas. He was wild but he had a good heart. I liked Johnny very much but I didn't want to marry him. I took several trips to Jamaica to see him and he introduced me to everyone in his family. He started divorce proceedings from his wife, which was unheard of: the Reata men had their mistresses but they never got divorced. Johnny did, though; he was serious about me and wanted to get married.

One day he called my father and asked him to come out to the airport, Midway Airport in Chicago, to meet him. Johnny was waiting to catch a plane and he told Jack, "I really want to marry Peggy. I've got a lot of money, I'm taking more out of the country now. I'll give Peggy anything she wants. I'm going to buy a ranch in the Southwest." Johnny was dashing and gorgeous with a gleaming white smile and silky black hair, but he was naive; he was too trusting of people, and even I could see that he was heading for a fall. He loved Jimmy; he would pretend he was a lion and put Jimmy on his back and play with him, do things that Rudy never did.

"Peggy, marry me," Johnny begged. "You'll make an honest man out of me and keep me on the straight and narrow." I didn't want to keep anyone on the straight and narrow. I was still longing for that house and normal life, and I turned down Johnny's proposal several times.

Buck had moved to Los Angeles when he got out of the service, he and Laura Mae had gotten a divorce, and he was building houses in the San Fernando Valley. Johnny decided to go out to California and I told Buck to help him out, to introduce him to some girls and show him around, which Buck did. I'd get phone calls from Johnny in the middle of the night, when he probably had a girl in the next room, and he'd say, "I miss you so much." I just laughed and told him to have a good time and to take care of himself.

He didn't do a very good job, though, because he got taken to the cleaners with his investments in Las Vegas. Johnny called one day a few months later and said, "Can I borrow a hundred dollars? I lost all my money and I have to go home to Jamaica." My father loaned him some money, which Johnny repaid many times over; he went back to the family business. The mob took him like crazy, cleaned him out. He wrote me long, mournful letters: "Why weren't you with me, Peg? You could have helped me. I wouldn't have gone so crazy if you'd been there." I'd hurt him very much, he said, by turning him down. A year or so later he called me and said, "Guess what? I've got a very fine job, totally on the up and up. My headquarters are in Mexico City. Have you ever been to Mexico?"

So I went down to Mexico, and on the plane from Chicago I met a nice guy who was in the furniture business in Minneapolis. We had a pleasant conversation and I could see that he was very attracted to me. When we got to Mexico City and he saw that I was greeted by a handsome man with a long limousine filled with flowers, he said, "Who are you anyway?" I said goodbye to the man from Minneapolis and took off with Johnny. He had our trip all planned, he was going to show me all of Mexico. The first night he took me to the Del Prado, where a suite had been reserved, and after dinner Johnny got deathly ill. The next day I had to put him in the hospital; he had pneumonia. "Here, Peggy," he said, "take this money. Go have a good time. I'm sorry, but I'll have to catch up with you." I told Johnny that I'd stay and look after him but he said no, he insisted that I go on to Acapulco alone. So I did.

In the hotel lobby in Acapulco I ran into the furniture man from Minneapolis. We started going around together and had a ball. I liked him, he was a sweet guy, but when I kissed him it just went flat, nothing. He proposed to me within a week, offered me my dream, the house in the suburbs, my son would have a father, all that. But when he kissed me I just couldn't stand it. I strung him along for a while, trying to decide if I should do it. I went back and saw Johnny in Mexico City—he was still in the hospital, poor guy—and he said, "Do you have any money left from what I gave you?" And I said no. I kissed him goodbye and flew back to Chicago with the furniture man.

I went up to Minneapolis with him to meet his family, but it didn't work out. I took off with one of his friends, I didn't care, and didn't come back for a week. I figured that that ended the relationship but he tried to see me again, and I said no. I was bitter; I was angry, disappointed still about my divorce, and I hadn't realized it. Johnny was nice and so was the man from Minneapolis, but I wanted something else. I didn't trust anyone and was incapable of giving any man a fair chance.

I went home to Chicago and Jimmy said, "Mommy, you look so beautiful!" I was sun-tanned, wore my naturally red hair long under big, wide-brimmed hats, my teeth sparkled; but my looks were deceptive, it was all show and for nothing. I wasn't really open to anybody. I felt guilty about having left Jimmy with my parents so much. He and my father had a wonderful relationship. It was such a beautiful sight to look out the window and see this old man walking hand in hand with a little boy. Jimmy was a gorgeous boy, with blue eyes and long blond curly hair; but he always had such a serious expression on his face. I'd neglected him, I knew it, but I felt lost. Underneath my pretty smile was a sad girl who felt like shutting off the world.

I settled down after the Mexico and Minneapolis jaunts. I worked at the Merchandise Mart one day a week and spent more time with Jimmy and my mother, who was confined to bed most of the time. I went out on dates occasionally, keeping my distance from romantic involvement. Then one evening at the Merchandise Mart I ran into Sam Stetson, a fellow I'd known for a few years and hadn't seen since I divorced Rudy. I'd had a mild, schoolgirl kind of crush on Sam ever since we'd met, and I was glad to see him.

Sam was very tall, a big, goodlooking Irishman who, in partnership with his father and brother, owned a large wholesale vegetable business on South Water Market Street in Chicago. Rudy had done some business with Sam's father and we used to go down to the produce market and have a drink with the boys at three or four in the morning. Those men stayed alive by drinking whiskey. It was a tough job and they were just getting started to work when Rudy and I were about to go home to bed. It was so damp and cold in the produce plant that I couldn't stop shivering and had to have Rudy hold the shotglass up to my lips because my hand was too shakey.

Sam and his younger brother, Randy, ran the business now. Randy was a smart kid, a cute, tough little guy who was disowned by their mother because he married an ex-prostitute. The marriage turned out well, however, and they had several children. Sam was a momma's boy, the Beau Brummel who dressed impeccably and always dined at the Pump Room or another fine restaurant. Sam's mother was always buying him a pair of socks or a cashmere sweater, and every year made him trade in last year's Cadillac so that she could buy him a new one. He was a spoiled son who could do no wrong so far as his mother was concerned.

Sam was very nice to me and asked me out. We began to see each other fairly regularly, though he still had his other girlfriends. He went around with some Chinese and Japanese girls and who knows who else, but I fell in love with Sam, I really did. If he called and I already had a date, I'd break it. He asked me to go with him to Palm Springs but I said no, even though I was dying to, because I thought that perhaps one day we'd get married, and I didn't think it was right. I didn't want a fling with Sam, that's not how I felt about him. I didn't want to have the reputation of being just one of his girls.

After a while, though, I could see that Sam wasn't ready to get married; he was having too good a time, he didn't want to be tied down. His mother thought he was too good for any woman and he stayed close to her; he never moved away from home until after she died. So Sam and I remained friends, and I saw him throughout my life in Chicago, here and there over the years. We always kept up on one another. Every Thanksgiving, which is my birthday, Sam would call up and say, "Hello, Turkey Baby. Do you need anything? How are you doing? What do you need for the table?" Sam was nice but he didn't want to settle down, and he didn't want to have anything to do with children. I would go out with Sam for a day, a Saturday night or a Sunday afternoon, but that was all. It was never going to go anywhere. We remained good friends and we'd tell each other our troubles, until a few years ago when he had a stroke and died. He never did marry.

Through Sam I met a man named Dominic Kress, an older gentleman from Michigan who owned a large manufacturing firm in Grand Rapids. He was a widower and he supported his mother, who was crippled from arthritis. Dom was an interesting fellow: he wore a beret and smoked cigarettes in a long holder and had the largest sailing ship on the Great Lakes. Every year he participated in the Lake Michigan races and usually took first place. We were attracted to each other very much, I liked doing things with him. He taught me how to hunt and fish in the Michigan woods, and sometimes we'd take Jimmy along. Dom was fond of my parents and gave them a new television set, but he didn't care for Jimmy. Like Sam, Dom didn't want any kids around. He thought I babied Jimmy too much. One time when we were on the boat he told Jimmy to do something and Jimmy froze, he wouldn't do it. Since that time I could feel that Dom didn't like Jimmy, and that complicated things.

I accompanied Dom on trips to New York and California, weekenders, and always had a good time. In Los Angeles with Dom, staying at the Ambassador, I was approached by an older woman who introduced herself as the sister of Sid Grauman, the owner of Grauman's Chinese Theater. "That's my brother over there," she said, pointing to a man sitting in a Rolls Royce parked at the curb in front of the hotel. He smiled and waved at me. "He would like to take you for lunch today," said the sister. I said, "Thank Mr. Grauman for me, but I'm not available." "How about dinner?" she asked. "I'm sorry," I said, "but I'm with someone." "All right, dear," she said, "but if you change your mind just call this number," and she handed me a card.

A friend of Dom's who was a producer asked me if I'd like to have a make-up job at one of the studios and I said sure, why not. So they made me up and I thought they'd made me look like a freak; but the producer said that the make-up was necessary in order to be able to photograph properly. We were on the RKO lot and we went into the cafeteria and I was sitting there having lunch when a waiter brought me a note. They were filming Dillinger's life story and the note was from the star, Lawrence Tierney, who was sitting directly across from us on the other side of the room. The note said, "Can I meet you later for cocktails? Just say where and what time." Tierney was a big, handsome thug, a wild character who had a reputation as a brawler and boozer. I showed the note to the producer and he said, "That guy's no good, don't pay any attention to it." The producer asked me if I wanted to stay in Hollywood, to take a screen test, and I just laughed. "I have to go home to Chicago," I said, "to my little boy." "Bring him out here," he said. "You're a little skinny, though," said the producer, "we'd have to fatten you up, feed you milkshakes."

Dom asked me to go to Europe with him but my mother was too sick, I couldn't leave for any length of time; but I accompanied him to New York and saw him off on a ship that was sailing for England. The photograhers asked me to sit on the rail and wave to them, as if I were going, too, so I did; and the next day, there was my picture in the paper. I said goodbye to Dom and he had one of his men, his bodyguard, actually, put me on a plane back to Chicago. That was the last time I saw Dom. He went to live in Spain for a few years and sent me silk shawls and small presents for my mother and father. Then one day I saw his photo on the obituary page of the Chicago paper: he'd had a heart attack and died in Madrid. I was surprised that Dom had gone to live in Madrid because I knew the city was land-locked, there was no place for him to sail a boat.

I met people from time to time, men I enjoyed being with but nobody in whom I was seriously interested other than Sam Stetson, and he was determined to remain single. I stayed home with my parents and Jimmy, but I felt that Jimmy was missing a father, that he needed to have a man around. My father loved Jimmy, they were pals, but he was old, and Rudy didn't have any time for his son. I thought that I should look around and find another husband, for Jimmy's sake if not my own.

I was introduced at a dinner party to a fellow named Michael Patrick Cohan, who said he was a great-nephew of George M. Cohan, the dancer, singer and actor. There was no reason for me not to believe him. Mickey, as he preferred to be called, was a great talker, totally believable, and as handsome and charming an Irishman as I'd ever met. Mickey spoke with a slight brogue and had excellent manners as well as being highly intelligent. He was witty without being glib and knowledgeable about a wide variety of subjects. I went out with him a week later and when he met Jimmy his eyes lit up: the two of them hit it off right away. Mickey fell in love with Jimmy and said, "That's the kind of boy I'd like to have for a son." It was difficult not to be charmed by Mickey, and on our second date he proposed marriage to me.

Originally from the East, Mickey was ten years older than I was, but extremely youthful in appearance. He worked as a sales representative for a steel firm located in Chicago. Mickey told me that he'd been injured in the war, leaving him with slightly defective vision; he did not have to wear glasses, he said, but he could never drive a car. So we took taxis, or I drove. He just could not see properly, though his hazel eyes betrayed no sign of injury.

I didn't want to rush into anything. I was impressed by Mickey's rapport with Jimmy, but for about a year and a half I dated other men as well. I had another boyfriend named Artie Howard, an acquaintance of Rudy's who ran a lounge, a small nightclub and bar called Aces and Eights. He gave Jimmy an electric train and used to let my dad sit around the place having drinks on the house. Artie wanted to marry me, too, and I liked him, but my mother absolutely forbade me to continue seeing him. She thought he was too much like Rudy and not as successful, and she was right. I still seemed to attract the night owls, the high life types, while what I thought I wanted was the plain, boy-next-door type.

Mickey told me that he'd been married once before but that he'd never had any children. His wife had been a buyer for a chain of ladies' apparel shops, and for whatever reason the marriage did not last very long. My mother was bedridden at this time, and I'd been sticking close to home. One night I went out on a date with Mickey and when we got back to the house Rose was in a coma. My father was asleep and hadn't noticed her condition, so we rushed her to the hospital. She regained consciousness only briefly the next day, and she died. My father was in disbelief; he hadn't realized just how sick my mother really was.

There was a large gathering at the funeral. All of Rose's old friends from Prairie Park, from the church, and all the family members were there. There were more flowers than I'd ever seen before, more than I'd been sent when Jimmy was born. The largest wreath was from Rudy, who stood by me during the burial. The night after Rose's funeral Jimmy and I were sitting on her bed, looking over the condolence cards, starting to write thank you notes, when the golden moth appeared at her window. It knocked itself against the glass, trying to get in, to get at the warmth of the light; and we sat there mesmerized by its beauty, the orange-gold colorings on its giant wings. The moth seemed to be flaming, brightening as we watched it. I wasn't sure what to do, it frightened me, so I turned off the lamp. Jimmy and I sat and waited in the darkness for thirty minutes before I turned the light back on. The moth was gone, and Jimmy looked at me with the most beautiful, innocent expression, and asked, "Was that Nanny?" I just told him that I didn't know for certain; it might have been a sign from Nanny, I said, that she was thinking of us and that she's safe in heaven.

Before she passed away, my mother told her sister, my Aunt Lilia, "I hope Peggy doesn't marry Mickey. There's something not quite right about him." Lilia told me this not long after Rose's funeral, but I didn't share her caution. Mickey was a great comfort to me, a sensitive, consoling presence; foolishly, I ignored my mother's intuition. I saw Mickey constantly; he took my father to the fights, solidified his camaraderie with Jimmy. Two months after my mother's death I married Mickey.

We had a quiet wedding, inviting only the immediate family and my Aunt Lilia, her husband Edgar, and their daughter, Natalie. We all had dinner together and in the garden-like entranceway to the restaurant was an old woman fortune-teller sitting at a card table. When she learned that it was my wedding day the old lady came over to our table and asked if I would like her to read my palm. I agreed to let her and she looked very seriously at my hand. She tried to tell me something good but she said she was having trouble getting a reading. She had to give up, dismissing my attempt to pay her.

I don't know what the fortune-teller saw, or didn't see, but three days after the wedding Mickey lost his job and the next day he would not get out of bed. He was in a trance: he wouldn't eat, drink or sleep. Mickey didn't move, he just lay there staring straight ahead. I called his boss at the steel company and found out that Mickey had been fired because of frequent absences. He had been on probationary status at his job, anyway, because of his psychiatric problem, I was told. I didn't understand, I said. What psychiatric problem? The boss explained to me that Mickey's war injuries caused him to go into catatonic states like the one he was experiencing now. Sometimes these seizures lasted days, sometimes only hours. Mickey was a bright guy, his former boss said, but the company needed a man they could depend on.

I was shocked that Mickey hadn't confided in me about his condition, and suprised that he'd been able to conceal it from me for the more than a year and a half I'd known him. He recovered from this attack and started looking for another job. I tried to be a good wife and kept house, and my dad, who was living with us—Mickey had moved into my house—was still working and contributing to our support. In fact, after Mickey lost his steel company job, my father was the sole suport of the household. I'd given up my one day a week work at the Merchandise Mart and was devoting all of my time to being a housewife and mother to Jimmy.

Mickey couldn't find a job, and he began spending more and more time away from the house. I didn't know where he was during the day or night. He would come home bedraggled and forlorn-looking and just flop on the bed. I was heartbroken; my dream of a nice home and husband and family was being shot down again. Things got so bad that I got in touch with Mickey's sister, Helen, who was living in West Virginia. She had written after the wedding, saying that she hoped Mickey would settle down now. She hoped he'd found a good girl and that he would be happy. Helen told me that she and Mickey were not related to the Broadway Cohan family, that Mickey had made all that up. She was horrified that he had not told me about his mental troubles since the war and said that I should get in touch with the Veteran's hospital in Chicago to which Mickey had been assigned.

I contacted the hospital and located the doctor under whose care Mickey had been. The doctor told me to bring him in as soon as possible, and that night I drove Mickey to the hospital. He didn't want to go, he begged me not to make him go back there; but I told him unless he submitted to treatment we were through. Mickey stayed in the hospital for a month and when he came out he seemed fine; his spirits were up and he promised me that everything would be all right. Within one week Mickey found a good paying job for another steel company. My father and I were amazed at Mickey's resiliency, he was like another person.

Mickey worked at his new job for six months without any problems. He was very good to Jimmy, who was growing up into quite a little athlete. Mickey and he would play football and baseball and go to ball games together. Mickey treated Jimmy like a boy should be treated, with plenty of affection and responsible guidance. When Jimmy went away to camp for the summer it was Mickey who wrote letters and cards to him, not Rudy. I regained my optimism when I saw the delight both Jimmy and Mickey took in their relationship.

My father had a heart attack from which he recovered quite rapidly but the doctors felt that he should get away from Chicago for awhile, away from the temptation to go to work. Buck had just moved back to town and he agreed to send me and Jimmy and Jack to Florida to live until Jack had recovered sufficiently. Mickey said that he would share the cost of our support with Buck, and so we moved down to Key West.

We lived in a beautiful hotel with a private beach. Jimmy and I went swimming, sailing and fishing and enjoyed ouselves tremendously. My father took long walks around the island and built up his strength; he had resisted the move but acknowledged that he was glad to be away from Chicago's severe winter weather. Mickey came down every couple of weeks, much as Rudy had when my mother and I had lived in Miami, and at first he seemed to be doing fine. I soon noticed something wrong, however, in Mickey's behavior: he never wanted to join the festivities at night. He would have dinner downstairs, but as soon as the dancing or any other activities began he would insist that we go upstairs to our room. He didn't want me to dance or talk with anybody else. I couldn't help but feel that there was something more than jealousy involved. I'd say, "But I like to dance. It's all right if you don't want to, sit and watch. I'm not going to go off with anyone else." Mickey did not like to dance, he wasn't a good dancer, which didn't really matter all that much to me, but he did not want me out of his sight while he was in Key West. "You stay right here with me," he'd say.

Mickey would take Jimmy out fishing for hours. They'd get in a boat and be way out in the ocean all day; they caught kingfish, mackerel, sailfish, shark, everything. Jimmy would bring his favorite fish of the day, one he'd caught, into the hotel kitchen and have the chef cook it for dinner. He couldn't have had a better time. I mentioned to my father that Mickey's behavior with me was a little odd, but Jack saw how much Jimmy liked him and told me to be patient, to give Mickey a chance.

After close to a year in Key West my father, Jimmy and I returned to Chicago. Mickey didn't tell me, but he'd been let go from his job some time before. I don't know where he got the money he'd been sending to us in Florida. Very shortly after our return, Mickey had another attack of catatonia, and again I had him placed in the Veteran's hospital.

I went to my brother for advice and help. I told Buck that I wanted to get free of Mickey. I explained that I had very little money left in trust from my mother and I wanted to get a divorce in the event Mickey was declared to be entirely mentally unstable, in which case I would not be able to divorce him. Buck arranged it through a lawyer friend of his and I brought Mickey the divorce papers in the hospital. I begged him to sign them, which he did, reluctantly.

Mickey was in the VA hospital for several months, and when he got out he called and asked to see me and Jimmy. He was living in a dumpy hotel on the near North side and I met him in a nearby park. I didn't want to be alone with him; we sat on a bench and watched Jimmy play on the swings and climbing bars. Mickey was unshaven, unkempt, and he scared me a little. He asked me for another chance, promising that he'd get back on his feet and get a good job. But I could see that he was wiped out; he was not the same person after his most recent spell. That was the last time I ever saw Mickey Cohan. It had been a very unhappy year and a half of my life, and I hardly knew what to think about it.

Aunt Lilia's daughter, my cousin Natalie, came to see me and said that she knew a nice fellow, a musician, a young man who had never been married, to whom she would like to introduce me. This was only a month after Mickey's release from the hospital, and I was still gunshy regarding men. I had gone back to work at the Merchandise Mart, four days a week now, Jimmy was able to take care of himself a little more, and I was beginning to enjoy my life again. The episode with Mickey had been a traumatic one, and I was very slowly coming out of shock. I hadn't been dating, only allowing myself an occasional dinner with Sam or one of the fellows from work. I liked the feeling of being home in the evenings and on the weekends with my son and my father, who had resumed his full work routine and was back on his feet. I thanked Natalie for her offer, but turned it down; I needed more time to digest this most recent experience and figure out how to carry on.

I began to think more seriously about the behavior of the men I had known. Dan O'Rourke had meant nothing to me, he hadn't really influenced or affected me in any way that I could discern. My father, Jack, had always been a hard worker, but a philanderer. He always had his girlfriends, even when he was married to my mother. This upset me toward the end of my mother's life, but Rose, who knew she was dying, said to me, "Let him enjoy himself, Peggy. It's all right, let him have a good time." One night, while my mother was still alive, I received a phone call from a man telling me to come right over to Jack's office; he'd had a heart attack during an all-night poker game. I rushed over and found my father lying on the floor. As I was coming in the other men were hustling girls out. I got my father to the hospital and he was taken care of, but I wondered why Jack carried on the way he did. Why did he do this to himself? Especially when he knew he had to be careful and take better care of his health.

During the time I was married to Rudy and my mother and I had the house in Miami, my father was expected one Thanksgiving weekend. Rudy arrived without him and said that Jack had told him he was making separate arrangements, that he'd see him down there. That Saturday we received a wire from the middle of the Atlantic Ocean where my father was aboard the *Queen Mary* on his way to England. He'd decided to take off and visit his old haunts in London. He went on to Berlin and Budapest and then went to Paris where he played in a bridge tournament. By the time he arrived in New York he had a gall bladder attack from too much rich food and high living and had to stay with and be taken care of by my Aunt Maria. My mother took a train up to New York from Miami to see that he was all right, and then brought Jack back to Chicago. Jack was a *bon vivant,* he loved going out on the town and he loved the ladies. I suppose some of his taste for life was passed on to me: He made a living but no fortune, preferring to spend his time enjoying himself. I loved him but didn't understand him until after his death. I didn't think Jack had treated Rose very well, and that colored my perspective.

Rudy was the boss. He knew best and it was best for whomever he was dealing with to accept that fact and act accordingly. I respected his forthrightness and his ability to make money but I could not surrender myself to his old country concept of the woman staying quietly in the background. Rudy and my father wanted me to be nothing more than a beautiful object, a showpiece, to be present only when it suited their purpose. Both of them had great spirit and self-confidence and I admired that; I often wished that I had the same ability to get things done. Buck was the same way, and I loved him dearly and always looked up to him: my handsome, older brother. But Buck went his own way. He was generous to me, helped me when I asked him to, but he was caught up in his own vision of himself in the world. Buck McCloud the Adventurer, the Architect, the Sailor, the Deep Sea Fisherman, the Great Lover. I was just Pretty Little Peggy to Buck. There was no reason for him to think of me in any other way, I suppose, but as with Rudy and my father it seemed that I was not given credit for being a whole person. Perhaps if I had lived up to a different set of expectations, my own, rather than down to their vision of what my role ought to be, things would have been different.

Mickey, of course, was no influence at all. Sam Stetson and the other men friends I had weren't of any real help to me in developing a valid sense of who I was. Kozeny, Rudy, Sam—they were only too happy to provide for me, take care of me, so long as I conformed to their idea of how a woman should behave. What I wanted, I thought, was rather modest; yet none of the men I had known were willing to share that kind of life with me. It all seemed so crazy. Other women I knew had managed to establish what I considered to be normal lives. Why was I so different?

Natalie kept after me to meet her musician friend, Andy Golden. After a few weeks of her well-intentioned pestering, I finally said all right, have him call me, and he did. I went out with him for coffee one evening and he told me all about himself. Andy was a Jew, but he didn't look at all Jewish: he had blond hair, blue eyes and a snub nose. He was the youngest of six brothers and sisters, all of whom were married and lived in Chicago, in the same neighborhood in which they had been raised. His father was dead but his mother, Sadie, was still alive. She lived in her own apartment near her children, each of whom contributed to her support, though her husband, who had been a boilermaker, had left her some money. Andy, the baby of the family, was her favorite.

Andy was in his mid-thirties. He had been an amateur boxing champion, and had put himself through college by playing the trumpet in dance bands. At the time I met him he was still making his living by playing in an orchestra, an "all-Latin" band in which he was the only non-Latin: Luis Camarones and his High Hat Rhumba Boys. We got along well enough and we went out on coffee and sandwich dates. It was a nice change for me not to be taken out in a Cadillac; Andy drove a beat-up, eight-year-old Buick.

We would go to a neighborhood restaurant for corned beef sandwiches or his apartment to listen to opera and jazz records.

Quite a change from El Morocco and the Chez Paree! Andy invited me down to listen to him play at various hotels for weddings and private parties, and I was impressed by his musicianship. I asked him why he hadn't gone to New York or Los Angeles and become a studio musician or led a band of his own on the nightclub circuit, and he said that he liked Chicago; it was his home, he was comfortable there, near his family. He really didn't like the rat race, he told me, the competition, especially when it came to music, which was his great love. I respected his attitude and what I interpreted as his ability to do what he wanted to do. He played occasionally for local radio programs and gave lessons on the side, though the rhumba band paid him a decent wage.

I discovered that Andy wanted the same things I did: a quiet life in his own home. I met Sadie, his mother, and found her to be a delightful woman. Now an overweight old lady, I could see that she had once been a beauty; Andy had gotten his coloring from her. She and her husband had lived in Hartford, Connecticut, for many years, and had moved to Chicago a few years before Andy was born. Sadie spent her time going to the synagogue and visiting with her lady friends. She was highly intelligent and generous with her time and money. We liked each other immediately and she told me it was time that Andy got married and made a family.

Andy was non-committal about Jimmy. His sisters, whom I liked, too, were all happily married; but they told me that Andy had never cared for their children, he couldn't stand having them around. They said that he had always been fussy about his things, his possessions, not wanting the children to touch anything that belonged to him. This seemed strange to me because Andy was not exactly a tidy person, his apartment was always messy.

Unlike Mickey and Rudy, Andy was an excellent dancer; dancing was one thing he really enjoyed doing. We started going out together on a regular basis, usually to small clubs that had a good dance band, most of whose musicians were friends of Andy's. He thought that I was the most glamorous woman he had ever seen. I was looking good at that point, my eczema was in a dormant stage, and I was out from under the cloud of my unfortunate marriage to Mickey. I had many fine things, furs and jewelry from my father and Rudy, and this impressed Andy. He thought that I was a rich girl but I straightened him out about that, telling him that I had to work to support myself and my son. I had never been poor, I explained. I had been raised in excellent circumstances financially, and my first husband had been a marvelous provider, but times had changed. I could see that Andy did not quite believe me; he was convinced that I was better off than I was.

Sadie pressed him to propose to me; she desperately wanted Andy to get married. Andy had fallen in love with me and whenever I went out on a date with another fellow Andy would sit under a tree across the street from my house waiting for me to come home. He'd wait there to see how long my date would stay in the hallway, or whether or not I would invite him in. I really wasn't interested in anyone else, but I did not yet want to limit myself to one person. Andy intrigued me; though he wasn't what I considered a handsome man, he was very smart and a relaxing conversationalist. We would sit and talk quietly for hours, something I had never done with Rudy. Andy admitted that he didn't have enough money to buy a house, and I said that I had my parents' place, where I lived, and had my father to take care of. I made it clear that if I were to marry again I could not abandon my dad.

Jimmy was now almost ten years old, and when I asked him what he thought about my marrying again he said that he liked our life the way it was: him, me and "Pops," which was his name for my father. My dad always called Jimmy "Babe." In the year or so before his death, however, Pops would often confuse Jimmy with my brother and call him Buck. Jimmy and his Pops had a very special relationship: they both enjoyed sports and my father knew the name of every baseball player that had ever played, which impressed Jimmy no end. They spent hours together watching ball games on television and playing cards. Jimmy loved to go down to the fur shop on State Street and help the old men cut up pelts. I realized that I hadn't really thought very much about how the experience with Mickey had affected Jimmy. He was spending more and more time with Rudy, who had recently remarried and was living not too far from us, and I felt that Andy's presence in the household, as far as Jimmy was concerned, could be no worse than a benign one. Even if Andy would not be the kind of ideal father for a boy Mickey had been, or could have been had he not been injured, at least Jimmy would still have Rudy and Pops around.

I loved Andy because he was easy-going and down to earth. I'd had enough of the flashy life, I decided, and told Andy that I would marry him. He reacted to my decision with absolute astonishment; he was overjoyed, as, needless to say, was Sadie. Jimmy was not so pleased, I knew that, but I really did feel that things would work out well for a change.

Andy's mother insisted on paying for the wedding; it was her pleasure, she said, I'd made her the happiest woman in the world by marrying her son. At the wedding dinner Jimmy, having been coached by his Uncle Buck, made the first toast: "I would like to propose a toast to my new father," Jimmy said, "and my old mother." All of the guests laughed uproariously at Jimmy's malaprop tribute, and it was a fine party. Buck and my father both thought I'd made a good choice in Andy; he appeared to be a solid, dependable, hard-working guy. Andy giggled and chortled throughout the ceremony and during the party afterwards. He was absolutely elated to be married to me.

We went to Acapulco for our honeymoon, leaving Jimmy in the care of one of Andy's sisters. We did not go first class, as I always had before, but it was all right. I decided that I had begun the more modest phase of my life and it made sense. Andy handled himself well in Mexico; he spoke some Spanish, having learned it while working in the rhumba band. I was disappointed in Andy as a lover, however. Not that he wasn't affectionate, he was a warm and jolly person; but when it came to sex he just didn't have what it took. To Andy, sex was just a thing that passed in the night, which displeased me. Times are different now, but in those days I believed that in order to live with a man you had to marry him. Maybe I should have lived with these men for a while before deciding whether or not to marry them, but that was not how I had been raised to behave. I did sleep with men I liked without marrying them, but not often; and they generally were men with whom I could never picture myself spending the rest of my life.

About the third day in Acapulco I came down with a terrible burn on my face. I broke out all over with sun blisters and had to spend the next few days in our room, bathing my face with a medicinal lotion. I told Andy to go ahead and enjoy himself, to talk with the people we'd met at the hotel, which he was happy to do. Later, after I'd recovered sufficiently to go out in public again, I learned from these people that in my absence Andy had never spoken of me, only of his mother and her wonderful cooking. Andy had had ample opportunity to sample my cooking; I had to make dinner for Jimmy and my father anyway, so Andy often ate at our house. This perturbed me somewhat. One woman at the hotel asked me how long Andy and I had been married and I told her that this was our honeymoon. She seemed very surprised. "All he does is talk about his mother," she said.

After the honeymoon Andy went back to work in the band. He moved all of his things into my house and, at his insistence, I stopped working; he wanted to be the breadwinner. My father continued to contribute to the household, of course, paying half of the family expenses. I thought this was too great a sum for Jack to be putting in but Andy's income was erratic. When the band played regularly so was the money, otherwise Andy had to depend on private lessons and radio gigs, which were undependable.

We did not go out often, only once in a while to a movie and rarely to a restaurant. Andy was not a big spender, which I liked, but at home he liked to eat and go to sleep. Our conversations, which before the marriage had been so interesting and entertaining, ceased almost totally. All of a sudden Andy didn't seem to have much to say to me.

Jimmy was left to his own devices; at ten years old he was on his own. He got himself a job delivering food on his bicycle for a neighborhood Chinese restaurant, so he began to support himself. Andy never had two words for Jimmy and Jimmy didn't seem to mind; at least he never mentioned anything about Andy's lack of interest in him to me. Chicago was changing, the downtown area was not as grand as it had been when I was younger, but to Jimmy the Loop was still a great place. He discovered the library, the theaters, and roamed around the city exploring; his independence was very impressive. Rudy had had another child, a son, by his second wife, and Jimmy spent a considerable amount of time at their house. Rudy was proud of Jimmy, too, so I didn't worry over his relationship with Andy.

I was annoyed, however, at Andy's selfish attitude when it came to food. If he saw a better piece of meat on my plate, or the best piece of food in the pan, he would take it for himself. I realized that he had been a bachelor for a long time, and that he'd been spoiled by his mother, and I let it go; that was just the way he was. Andy had never been slim, but after our honeymoon he began to gain a great deal of weight. He seemed not to take the same care with his appearance as he had when I'd first met him, and that puzzled me. I noticed all of these things but chose not to dwell on them or let them disturb me. I was determined that the marriage should work.

Three months to the day after our return from Mexico I discovered that I was pregnant, which delighted me. Andy seemed quite pleased about it and I immediately began to hope for a girl. When I told Jimmy that I was going to have another child he just grinned and gave me a big kiss. "Don't worry, Ma," he said, "I'll take care of you."

I had a terrible pregnancy. I was sick for practically the entire nine months that I was pregnant, but I had a particularly difficult time around my sixth or seventh month. It was during the seventh month that a horrible incident occurred.

It happened on a Thursday afternoon. I remember that because Thursday was the day that I did the laundry. Jimmy was in school, my father was at work, and Andy was at a band rehearsal. It was late in spring, the weather was lovely and I had hung some of the smaller rugs on the line in the yard in order to air them out. I carried the big basket of dirty clothes down the back steps into the basement; this was getting more difficult to do as my stomach became larger. I was wearing a button-down apron type of dress that made me look hefty rather than pregnant. It made me look straight up and down, even though my stomach was quite pronounced by this time. I put the clothes into the washing machine and then decided to sweep up the basement a little bit.

I went into the coal room to get a broom and when I came out I noticed that the rest of the basement had gone dark. The washing machine light was out, too. I thought that there had been a short, that a circuit had overloaded somehow, and I went over to the fuse box to fix it. As I reached up to the box a giant arm came around my neck and another hand stuffed a gag in my mouth, a dirty pair of men's shorts. I tried to say something but just then I felt a blow across my belly and I collapsed to the floor. A man put his head close to my right ear and whispered, "Don't make a scene, don't scream. I won't hurt you. I just want to rob you."

I managed to spit out the gag and bit into his thumb as hard as I could. He immediately jabbed me in the side with a small knife. He jabbed me several more times but I felt no pain. Instead my mind was racing: I'm going to die today, I thought. How is Jimmy going to get into the house when he comes home from school? Oh my poor little boy, his mother will be dead. My thoughts were only of Jimmy, and my father, too.

The attacker got my hands bound tightly behind me, then tried to stuff this vile pair of filthy shorts into my mouth again. I held a piece of them in my teeth and pretended that I was choking. He took another foul-smelling rag and put it around my head so that I could not see him. I did sense, however, that he was very young. He didn't smell of tobacco or alcohol or anything else that I could identify. Being pregnant, my senses were especially keen to odors, but this man had no telltale scent.

He dragged me into the coal room and left me lying on the coal pile. He must have been wearing workman's shoes with soft rubber soles because I heard him pad away, climbing the stairs to the house. For a while I couldn't hear any noise. I thought, fine, let him take anything he wants from the house, I don't care about that. Whatever he wants let him take it and go on his way; I didn't want him there when Jimmy came home from school. Then I heard him come back down the steps and over to me. He didn't say a word.

He took me by the hair, my long, dark red hair, and dragged me the length of the basement, the entire length of that basement on my back. He tried to pull me up but I pretended for the moment that I had fainted. He dragged me to the bathroom in the front of the basement; he seemed to know his way around very well. The gag was still in my mouth, my eyes were covered, and I knew that he was going to rape me. He took one of my legs and tied it to a leg of the old-fashioned tub in the bathroom, lifted up the apron that I had over my dress, then tore open the buttons of the dress. When

95

he saw my big stomach he let out an awful groan. "Oh no," I heard him say.

It's surprising how one feels in a situation like that; I really did not have much feeling. He didn't rape me, but he took his sharp, little knife and started to cut me, making hundreds of small gashes all over my body. He must have gotten great pleasure out of this, because all while he was doing it I could hear moaning sounds coming from deep in his throat. He must have had an orgasm. After he stopped cutting me I heard him wiping up the floor around me. I'll never forget that wiping sound for as long as I live.

While he carved and moaned and wiped I pretended to be absolutely dead, totally collapsed. When he finished wiping he got up and left me on the bathroom floor, closing the door behind him as he went out. The next thing I heard was him walking up the stairs into the house again. I heard drawers being opened and closed; opening and closing, opening and closing. It seemed to go on for an eternity; then I really did pass out.

When I came to I shot the gag out of my mouth and started to yell. I screamed and screamed as loud and as long as I could. I didn't want Jimmy to come home and find me tied up on the floor. I had no feeling in my hands or arms. I was lying on my hands, which were still tightly bound; I couldn't get them loose. Finally I managed to sit up, to push myself up against the bathtub. I twisted around and the bag-like rag fell off of my head. That was when I saw that it had been a pair of dirty shorts that he'd stuffed into my mouth. There was blood around me on the floor. I scrunched my body over and with my teeth managed to undo the tie around my ankle and the tub leg. The rope was still curling as I got up.

I screamed and screamed and at last I heard footsteps, someone running into the basement through the backyard. I hoped it wasn't Jimmy; I knew that it must be after school by now. I had no feeling in my wrists and one arm. I wanted my hands to be free but I couldn't loosen the tie. I heard a woman's voice calling, "Peggy!

Peggy! Is that you? Peggy, where are you?" "In here," I yelled. "In the bathroom!" It was my neighbor, Florence O'Malley, who opened the door and found me. I sat on the edge of the tub and buried my head in her chest. I was a mess, and Florence started to cry. She untied my hands and helped me up the stairs into the house. I fell on the couch in the living room and half passed out.

Florence called my obstetrician, whose office was only a few blocks away, and told him to come right over; then she phoned the police. The doctor got there before the police and he gave me a shot of penicillin; then he had Florence run me a warm bath and they put me into it. I was not hysterical. I told them both what happened very calmly and quietly. They got me bathed and dressed before the police arrived.

The doctor told them that I was in shock, but mildly so; he told me there had been no damage to the baby, and I was greatly relieved. He said that was because I had not gotten overexcited during the attack. I had remained very cool under the circumstances, which was surprising, especially to me. I told the police what the man had done, that he had worn workman's shoes and khaki or green colored workman's pants; I'd only seen the cuffs and bottom part of his trousers. He'd pressed his face against mine when he first grabbed me so that I knew he was clean-shaven, and that he did not smoke. The police told me that there had been a series of attacks similar to this one made in the neighborhood recently. Apparently this guy watched for women to go down into their basements alone to do the wash, and then assaulted them. I was the first, they said, that had not been raped; being so pregnant had at least spared me that.

Florence had also called Andy and my father. Jack came home right away. He took it very hard, and cried. He was very kind and sympathetic, which surprised me a little bit. I was stiff from all of my bruises and the cuts, but I acted very light about the whole thing; I was already trying to forget it. Andy thought it was horrible but he didn't say much. All of us tried to keep it light in front of Jimmy, who, fortunately, was late coming home from school that day; he'd stopped to play ball at the park. It was a good thing that he had because apparently the man who had attacked me had beaten and raped other women while their children were around.

The police took away my bloody clothes for lab tests. When the case was over they called and asked me if I wanted them back and I told them no, to please burn them. The doctor gave me a sleeping pill and when I awoke I felt fine mentally but not physically. I checked to see what might have been taken from the house and was surprised to see a hundred dollar bill I had left on my dresser to pay the coal bill was still there, on my perfume tray. Gone were some panties, lingerie, and my house keys, but nothing else that I could see. Various detectives came to see me over the next several weeks, and one of them, an expert in psychology, told me that he had been following the case closely. He was really out to get this maniac.

The next day I went back into the basement and cleaned all of the white fingerprint powder off of the walls and doorknobs. I had to laugh, though it was painful, to see that the wash was still in the machine. Nobody had bothered to finish doing the laundry for me! A day or two later I received a crank phone call. I didn't think much about it at first and just hung up. But then I began to get them regularly, usually around five o'clock in the afternoon. I alerted the detective assigned to my case and he happened to be at the house one afternoon when the call came. These calls were really rude, vicious, mean tirades. The caller was a man, but there was no overt sexual content to what he said. While the cop was there I kept the caller on the line and made a date to meet him at a rooming house on the near North side.

The detective went to the meeting place instead of me and found an old man who was an employee with the gas company. They roughed him up, I guess, and asked him why he had been harassing me. "Oh," he said, "she was an attractive lady who was always very nice to me when I came over to read the meter. She would ask me if I was all right, how my arthritis was. She was always very solicitous, very nice, and I always dreamed about her."

All of this happened during my seventh month of pregnancy. My father had to have a cataract operation at this time, too, which brought on a heart atack; so I was running out to the hospital to see him almost every day for three weeks. Meanwhile, the detectives kept in touch with me regarding the rapist. One day they called and told me that they had captured him while he was attempting to rape another woman in the neighborhood. They did not need me to testify, they said; they had plenty of other witnesses. He was twenty-two years old, a student at the University of Chicago who was majoring in psychology! He was a part-time construction worker, which explained the work shoes and pants. His name was Stewart Terry; a bright young man with a bolt loose. Terry was convicted—they'd found my keys and all of the other ladies' keys in his apartment—and sent to jail. He was out on good behavior nine months later.

Shortly after his release from prison a woman was attacked early one morning in Lincoln Park and had her head cut off. A man happened to be looking out of his window across from the park at the lake through field glasses and saw something being pulled into the bushes: it turned out to be this woman. She had been the owner of a beauty parlor who was walking to work when Stewart Terry attacked her, raping and murdering and decapitating her. The police knew it was Terry because of fingerprints on the body and he was indicted for the crime. He'd really gone off the deep end this time. Terry had a shrewd lawyer, however, and he managed to get Terry off.

After this acquittal I began to be a little fearful, especially walking home alone in the dark. One of the detectives who had been assigned to my case called me and said, "Don't worry, we're going to get this guy one of these days soon." His telling me this did not really put my mind at ease; they'd caught Terry twice now, once for a grisly murder, and he was still walking around loose.

But shortly thereafter I received another call from this same detective. "Stewart Terry is dead," he told me. "We shot him while he was entering a girl's apartment through a window. We didn't have to shoot him," he said, "we could have captured him. But we thought it best to get rid of him once and for all."

Two months after my ordeal with Stewart Terry my daughter Molly was born. I was thrilled to have a daughter; she was the most beautiful thing in the world to me, with her little round red face, big black eyes and full head of black hair. I was pleasantly surprised when two of the detectives who were working on the rape case came to the hospital to see Molly and to make sure that I was all right.

Actually, I had as miserable a delivery as I had a pregnancy. When I felt the contractions begin I told Andy, "This it it, it's time. Let's go." And he got so nervous that I barely got to the hospital on time. The nurse wanted to give me an enema and I told her to get away. The baby had started to come out by then and if I'd been given an enema I would have dropped Molly in the toilet. I had to stay in the hospital longer than I would have liked, a few days, because there were some complications as a result of the quick delivery. This made Andy worry about having a large bill to pay, and he asked me to come home as soon as possible.

For the year or so prior to Molly's birth, from about the time of my marriage to Andy, Rudy had become increasingly ill. He had cancer of the colon and rectum. Once while we were still married I saw blood in the toilet and I said to him, "You'd better take care of those hemhorroids." He said that he would, but he never did; and that was the beginning of his cancer that killed him before he was fifty years old. Jimmy hadn't really known just how sick his father was, and Rudy's death, two months after Molly was born, was quite a shock to him. He refused to go to school for days, preferring to stay in the backyard throwing a ball against the garage wall. Andy told him that he had to go back to school but Jimmy just ignored him, so I told Andy to leave him alone and let him deal with it in his own way.

Rudy's funeral was well-attended; hundreds of people were there, many I had not seen for ten years. Rudy's second wife, Dora, was a lovely girl from a poor family. She and I got along very well; neither of us cared for Rudy's sister, Irma, or his brother, Bruno. Both Irma and Bruno treated Jimmy like a poor relation, ostracizing him because of me, I suppose, because I was not Jewish. Jimmy once told me that Bruno had said to him, "Deep down inside ninety-five per cent of the Gentiles hate the Jews. You can't trust a Gentile." To Jimmy, this meant him, too, because he was only half Jewish, and not the half that counted. Jimmy didn't care, though, and after Rudy's death he never went to see Irma or Bruno.

Rudy's father, Ezra, was a fine man, however, and was as fond of me as I was of him. He was a tall, handsome Austrian with a big, old country mustache, who had been in the clothing business. Ezra was broken-hearted when Rudy died, and he passed away, too, not long after. I used to call him up in the old days, when Rudy was working late, and I'd say, "Come on, Pa, we're going out on the town." We'd go to the old German and Czechoslovakian and Russian restaurants and have a high old time. Ezra was very upset when Rudy and I divorced, but we remained good friends.

At Rudy's funeral Dora and I consoled each other. Jimmy remained tight-lipped and refused to speak to anybody. Irma carried on worse than anyone, fainting and swooning. Jimmy just stood there, stern faced, with his little brother, Willie, looking at the casket being lowered into the ground. I didn't realize at the time how seriously Jimmy was affected by his father's death. In the last few years Rudy had been very good to Jimmy, taking him on trips to Florida and New York, and encouraging him to hang around with him at the store. Jimmy knew all of Rudy's mob buddies, he liked being around these tough guys and sitting with his dad in restaurants and bars and nightclubs during the day, watching the showgirls rehearse. If there was anything positive about Rudy's premature death, I thought at the time, it was that Jimmy would not feel pressured to become a part of that life. The times were changing, anyway. Many of Rudy's pals were dying out or being found dead in the trunk of a car or weighted down in the Chicago river. The old guard was being moved out of Rush Street, the good old restaurants were closing down. There were no more big limousines lined up in front of the Club Alabam. That was gone.

Rudy had always had plenty of money, and I was sure that he had left Jimmy well provided for. At the funeral, however, Bruno told me that Rudy had not left a will, and I smelled a rat. Sure enough, with Bruno and his lawyers handling the estate, Jimmy was left out in the cold with nothing, and Dora and Willie practically so. Dora at least had the house and half of the pharmacy—Bruno owned the other half share—as the widow, those could not be taken away from her. Bruno claimed there was nothing else, that Rudy had left no cash, no other holdings, no provision for Jimmy. I asked Bruno about the hotel safety deposit boxes, the large amounts of cash Rudy always stashed away; but Bruno said there was nothing left, that times had been tough lately. I knew he was lying but there was nothing that I could do. Rudy had always trusted Bruno, his older brother, they were partners in everything, and I'm certain Bruno took it all.

Dora, however, was very good to Jimmy, and Jimmy liked her. She took Jimmy and Willie on a trip to New York a few months after Rudy's death, and showed them a good time. Dora married again a couple of years later, to the son of a friend of my father's, had two more children and always made sure that Jimmy was welcome in her house. Jimmy and Willie never lost touch with one another and they still see each other often. After attending their grandfather Ezra's funeral, both boys chose to have nothing further to do with Rudy's family and neither Dora nor I could blame them.

Andy decided that he couldn't take the uncertainty of the music business anymore and told me that he wanted to open a restaurant. Luis Camarones was moving to New York so that ended Andy's regular gig, and he did not want to depend on lessons and occasional work for an income. He knew that I had some money that my mother had left me and he asked me to loan it to him to start his own delicatessen. Andy said that he would be able to pay me back within a year, he was sure the place would be a success. He had secured a good location, he said, not too far from Rudy's drugstore. I gave Andy ten thousand dollars, practically all that Rose had left me.

I occupied my time with Molly, being a good mother, giving her lots of love and attention. My regret was that I hadn't given Jimmy the same attention. I hadn't known how to take care of a child properly when he was born, and I made up for it with Molly. Jimmy had always been slightly withdrawn, though he was very bright and a leader among his friends. He'd get into scrapes now and then, little things at school, and when I'd find out about them he'd say, "It's my business, Ma. There's nothing for you to worry about." He'd say this to me when he was seven years old. Jimmy was a remarkable boy, he learned to take care of himself early on in his life. I just told him that I was always there for anything if he needed me.

Molly kept me busy, and my housekeeping, but I was growing

increasingly dissatisfied with Andy. He didn't seem to care very much for Molly and never did a thing to help me around the house. Also, he wasn't bringing in any money from the restaurant; in fact, he asked me for another loan, but I told him I had nothing more to give him.

One afternoon I went to the opening of a new supermarket in the neighborhood with my neighbor, Florence O'Malley, the woman who had found me tied up in the basement. It was a nice warm day, the first time I'd left Molly with a sitter, who took her in her stroller to the park. Florence and I filled up my car with groceries at the store and when we parked in front of my house started to unload them from the trunk. Florence was walking up to the door of the house with one of the packages and I was on the street when a dusty old car drove up and stopped right next to me. The car was a dirty beige color, and inside were five men with long-visored fishermen's caps on their heads and handkerchiefs tied over their faces. The driver kept his hands on the steering wheel and the other four each pointed a gun at me. One of them said, "Okay, lady, hand it over!"

I was wearing a beautiful four-and-a-half carat, square-cut emerald ring and a six carat headlight diamond ring, both of which Rudy had given me. I didn't like to leave them at home, and thought it safer to wear them. I said to the men, "Here, take my purse, there's money in it." But they said, "No, we don't want that. Give us the rings." I started to argue with them. I must have been crazy because they were pointing these big guns at my face. Then I turned around and screamed at Florence, "Get the police! Florence, run for the cops! I'm being held up!" When she turned and saw what was happening, Florence fainted dead away on the sidewalk, spilling all of the canned goods out of the bag she was holding. I just stood there and watched the cans rolling down the walk over the curb. The robbers watched this happen, too; it was a ridiculous scene.

"Come on, lady!" the stick-up men shouted. "Give us the rings!" I told them that I couldn't get the diamond off my finger, that my finger had swollen; it was larger now and the diamond was on there permanently. "Okay," one of them said, "get her, Joe!" One of the guys got out of the car and stuck the barrel of his gun up against my cheek then drew it back as if he were going to hit me in the head, and I said, "All right, here, take them," and gave them both rings. I was afraid they might have cut my finger off in order to get the diamond. As they drove away I tried to get the license number but the car was covered with dust and dirt and I couldn't read it. The car or the plates had probably been stolen, anyway, I thought.

I ran over to Florence, who was still collapsed on the sidewalk, and revived her. "Oh, Peggy," she said, when she came to, "I'm so sorry. I was scared to death when I saw those guns. Did they shoot you?" I assured Florence that I was all right, that the robbers had taken my rings but hadn't hurt me. "Peggy," she said, "why do these terrible things happen to you?"

The rings had not been insured, so I was very disheartened by their loss. I helped Florence into my house, and we called the police. Jimmy came home and found the kitchen filled with cops standing around, drinking coffee. "Did you get attacked again, Ma?" he asked, and I told him what had happened. "Jesus, Mom," Jimmy said, "maybe you'd better hire a bodyguard." The police never did catch the robbers or recover my rings.

I suppose Andy did love Molly in his own way. Like Rudy he found it difficult to relate to a child before it could walk and talk. He felt no responsibility for Jimmy at all, even after Rudy's death. Andy never gave Jimmy the right time of day; he wasn't mean to him, he wasn't good to him. But Jimmy was no problem to me. He worked at his delivery job three days a week and concentrated on sports. He was developing into a fine athlete and joined various baseball leagues around the city. Jimmy did this all on his own. He bought his baseball gloves and basketballs with the money he earned himself.

Andy's sloppiness so enraged me one day that I told him he simply had to help me out around the house. My father was recovering from another heart attack, so I had him to care for, as well as the baby. When the oven at Andy's delicatessen went out he asked me to cook roasts for him at home, which I would then deliver to him downtown. My gas bills were tremendous. I had never really recovered from my miserable pregnancy and I was working too hard. I was having trouble with minor infections that nagged at me and my health was not good. After cooking a huge roast beef for Andy one morning I was carrying it out of the kitchen when I passed out in the dining room, falling on the floor, the roast tumbling out of the pan and the juices spilling all over the rug. Jimmy came running when he heard the noise and tried to lift me up. He thought for a moment that I had died because I didn't move. I was exhausted, both mentally and physically; things could not go on this way.

I informed Andy that I was through cooking for the delicatessen, I wouldn't do it anymore. He hadn't been bringing home any money for months. I'd had to borrow from Buck, who had just moved to Florida, in order to pay the bills. Buck was very generous to me, and knew that I had our father to take care of. Jimmy helped me with Molly, not Andy. Jimmy would diaper her and give her her bottle; when she vomited on the carpet next to her crib Jimmy scrubbed it out with a brush. I took great pleasure in my children, watching them. Those were my best moments during the time I lived with Andy.

Andy and I just were not getting along and finally he decided to live down in the back of his restaurant and keep later hours. I thought this was a good idea, and as soon as he left I knew I did not want him back in my house. I felt better after he was gone, and didn't mind doing the heavier chores around the house like shoveling coal into the boiler in the basement at five in the morning during the winter. After Andy moved out I remembered a time when Jimmy had been about four or five years old and we looked out the back window of the house into the yard and saw dozens of rats scampering around. They were crawling over Jimmy's fire truck and up the wall toward the windows. I grabbed a broom and knocked them down off the side of the house. I really thought they were going to jump through the window and bite us. We got rid of them by putting poison food balls in the yard. But I was struck by the thought of having rats coming into the house in the form of men. It seemed appropriate to me just then equating men with rats.

Before Andy left the house he and Jimmy got into a big fight. Jimmy came home one evening and heard Andy and me arguing. I guess he went into the kitchen and made some dinner for himself and listened to us arguing in the bedroom; there hadn't been many peaceful moments around the house lately. Finally Andy came out of the bedroom and Jimmy could hear me crying. Jimmy, who

109

was twelve years old when this happened, got up from the kitchen table and walked into the dining room, where Andy was standing, and pushed him as hard as he could. "Why don't you leave her alone?" Jimmy yelled. "Who are you to tell anybody anything? You're nothing but a forty-year-old failure!"

This really infuriated Andy. He was a strong guy, he'd been a boxer and a wrestler, and he grabbed Jimmy by the biceps and held him off the ground. I could see what was happening through the bedroom doorway and I thought Andy was going to crush Jimmy or throw him against the wall. Jimmy fought to free himself, but he couldn't, so he spit in Andy's face, over and over again. I didn't interfere, I couldn't say anything. Finally, Andy put Jimmy down and walked out of the house. "You shouldn't have called him that," I said to Jimmy. "Why not?" he said, and went into his room and shut the door.

I began to have difficulty breathing at night while I was married to Andy, and I went to a doctor who diagnosed my problem as emotional asthma. My nervous condition was now expressing itself as asthma rather than eczema. This doctor prescribed cortisone and filled his own prescriptions. The cortisone made me feel better but I started gaining weight. I blew up like a balloon. I lost my figure and varicose veins popped out of my legs. I wasn't able to function properly while I was on the cortisone, and it wasn't until after Andy moved out that I got off this horrible drug and back to normal.

Sadie, Andy's wonderful mother, was very upset about the separation. I saw her just before she died and she said, "Sweetheart, you don't look very happy. Is that bum son of mine bothering you? Just tell me and I'll take care of him." She was a sweet woman and I sincerely missed her after she passed away. I would bring Molly down to the delicatessen to see Andy, and he fussed over her more than he ever had when he lived with her. He still wasn't giving me any money and I didn't know what to do about that.

One day I came home and found a man waiting for me. "Your

110

husband sent me," he said. "I need money in a hurry or they're going to turn off the lights at his place. He has to get down to the electric company with a couple of hundred dollars immediately." I told him that I didn't have that much cash at the house; I couldn't give it to him. "If you don't give it to me," the man said, "Andy says you'll never get a dime out of him for your daughter." "What difference does it make?" I asked. "He's not giving me anything now anyway." The phone rang. It was Andy begging me to give him the money, swearing he'd pay me back. "What about the ten thousand, Andy?" I asked him. "Are you going to pay that back, too?" It had to stop, I told him. I had no more for him: no more money, no more me. It was over. I hung up the phone and told the man to get out.

That night I had second thoughts about what I'd done. I began to feel sorry for Andy, I knew he was working hard trying to make a go of it. So I left Molly with Jimmy and drove down to Andy's place taking all the cash I had—about a hundred and fifty dollars—with me to give to him for his electric bill. The lights were on in the delicatessen; the front door was open but there were no customers inside. I walked into the back, to the room where Andy slept, and found a little girl, about six years old, sleeping on his bed. Just then Andy came in with a woman, one of the strippers from a joint across the street. "What's going on here?" I asked him. Andy gave me a sheepish look and said nothing. The woman said, "Don't get excited. I'm a good friend of Andy's and he was just babysitting for my kid." I looked at Andy. "You wouldn't even babysit for your own daughter," I said, keeping my voice as even as possible. "You won't lift a finger to help me. You stole all of my money. And here I come down because I feel sorry for you to give you my last hundred dollars so that you can pay your electric bill. He's quite a guy, your good friend Andy," I said to the woman. "And he's all yours."

I filed for divorce the next day. I took Andy to court because I wanted child support, the amount of which Andy and I agreed upon in advance. I knew I probably didn't stand much of a chance

111

of collecting it but I wanted to have a way of possibly eventually recovering some of what he owed me. Andy represented himself and he talked so much that the judge had to rap his gavel and tell him to be quiet. Of course I had to pay for the divorce.

As I expected, Andy was constantly remiss regarding his child support payments. I would get two weeks payment, then six or seven weeks would pass before he'd send another check. I used to ask him what he expected me to use to pay for Molly's clothes, her doctor bills, her food. I hadn't asked for alimony, I didn't want anything for myself from Andy. It was both exhausting and demeaning to myself to have to nag him about the pittance he had agreed to send for his daughter.

Through an old friend of my mother's, a doctor, I found a job at a private hospital in Chicago as a receptionist. Dr. Marcus Edgewood was a pioneer in the field of heart surgery. He and my mother had been friends for forty years and he was only too glad to help me out. My basic duties at the hospital were to greet visitors and announce their arrival to the proper stations, but I gradually became more of an aide to Dr. Edgewood. Edgewood was close to eighty years old by the time I went to work for him, but he was still very active and the full-time director of medicine at the hospital. Open-heart surgery was just becoming an accepted practice and Edgewood was always flying off to Los Angeles or Houston or Boston to assist in an operation. I enjoyed my work and not having to depend on Andy for financial support.

Edgewood told me that he wanted me to keep an eye on activities at the hospital, to be, in effect, his spy. He travelled a great deal and needed someone he could trust. I became that person. Edgewood was unmarried at the time I went to work for him and I fixed him up on dates when I could. He was a fine-looking man who looked twenty years younger than he was. At a dinner one night at Dr. Edgewood's house I was introduced to a man named Lee Randolph, from Beverly Hills. Lee was in his fifties, the director of several companies having to do with film processing and related industries, who also bankrolled movies in Hollywood. It was as executive producer of a film called *Heart Doctor*, that he came into contact with Marcus Edgewood, who had acted as a technical adviser for the production. Lee was married but no longer lived with his wife. Much of his time was spent away from California, in Chicago and New York, in both of which cities he maintained an apartment. Under the watchful eye of Dr. Edgewood, Lee and I became close friends. It was a relationship that was very good for me at the time. My life was calm again and I was developing a new sense of security.

Jimmy helped me out tremendously with Molly, babysitting when I needed him to and fixing her meals. He was growing into a tall, handsome boy; he had quite a head for business, too. After graduating from grammar school, Jimmy got a job working every day after high school at a hot dog and hamburger shack in the neighborhood. He always had a pocketful of money, and between us we soon had no problem supporting our little household. My father decided to live in a residence hotel nearer his work. He was feeling good again, and he liked to see his lady friends. I used to ask them why they went around with my dad—he was so much older than most of them—and they would say, "Oh, Jack is so sweet. He treats a lady properly, with respect."

As soon as he was old enough to drive, Jimmy bought a motorcycle which he kept at a friend's house. He kept it over there, he said, because he didn't want to worry me—or listen to me telling him to be careful all the time. He had lots of girlfriends, whom he used to bring home now and then and introduce to me. Sometimes they would call up and ask me why Jimmy hadn't asked them out lately. He was developing along the lines of my father and brother but he was a good boy. Jimmy worked hard from the age of ten. I used to make him undress on the back porch when he came home from his hot dog job because he smelled so horribly from cooking French fries and Polish sausages and chopping onions. But he didn't mind working, and he did well in school, or well enough, and played ball, too. Jimmy was a hard-nosed kid, he knew the score. My only worry was little Molly, my dear little girl, and she was a happy, roly poly child.

A few months after I'd divorced Andy, Jimmy said to me, "You know, Ma, I don't think you should get married again. We do okay on our own." He was right, and I should have listened to him.

I was working full-time at the hospital and feeling good. Molly went to nursery school, and I found a nice woman in the neighborhood who would pick her up each day after school and stay with her until I came home in the late afternoon. I was slim again, I'd gotten my figure back. It was wonderful to have a man like Lee Randolph remember my birthday, take me out to the best restaurants and the theater. When Lee was not in town I went out with other men, including my friend Sam Stetson; but if Lee was in Chicago I didn't see anyone else. I had no expectations about eventually marrying Lee or anything like that. One reason I believe we got along so well is that each of us was just glad to be in one another's company, that's all. It was an ideal relationship for the time being.

This was a relaxed period in my life. I had money in my pocket and I enjoyed my job. I became more and more involved in the workings of the hospital. I took a course on medical terms and another on para-medical aid. Though my job was in reception and admitting I often helped out in the emergency room. I never would have thought that I could have assisted people who had been cut up or shot, women with burned babies; but I got very involved in whatever I was asked to do.

My own health was better than it had been in a long time. The asthma disappeared and I had no signs of the eczema that had plagued me throughout my life. A doctor at the hospital took care

116

of the varicose veins I'd gotten after Molly's birth. He gave me fifty shots in my legs and said, "Never gain weight and don't drink coffee and you'll never be bothered with varicose veins again."

Time was passing, pleasantly for a change. One weekend Lee flew me out to Los Angeles to accompany him to the Academy Awards ceremonies. We had a lovely time and I was back at work at the hospital in Chicago on Monday morning. I was having good times again, high times, but keeping a proper perspective on things. Lee would take me on a trip, buy me a string of pearls, but then I would go home, back to work, to Molly and Jimmy. I took things as they came. I needed to have control over my life and I was doing my best to maintain that position. Too many horrible things had happened for me to get carried away, to get involved with anything or anybody without seeing the situation clearly. My times had been either high or low, with very little in between. I realized that the past made very little sense to me.

Dr. Edgewood had encouraged me to keep an eye on things for him at the hospital, and I did. I knew what was going on in every department. I knew who was sleeping with whom, which doctor was cheating on his wife. I knew everybody's problems, and nurses and doctors would confide in me. Friends of mine would say, "Peggy, why don't you latch onto one of those nice single doctors?" But I didn't want to, I really didn't want to get married.

I formed a few close friendships with women who worked in the hospital, in the billing and insurance departments, but I never had very many women friends. I never liked to gossip. Women always looked at me like an outsider, and I think this had to do with my looks, the fact that I was prettier than most of them. It didn't make any difference to me, I was never stand-offish; but it was difficult for me to get along with most women. I made a great friend in an older Swedish woman named Ada who worked at the hospital. We spent holidays at each other's houses, went shopping together and to the movies. Ada adored Molly and often took care of her for me when I went out with Lee. She and I started going to fortune-tellers together and comparing forecasts. Ada was a great

117

gal, and it was a real blow to me when she died suddenly of a heart attack at the age of fifty. Ada's death shocked me because she hadn't been sick a day in her life; she was a big, strong Swede with a sharp sense of humor and a consistently optimistic outlook on life. I still miss her.

I never was one for organizations like the PTA. I had little or nothing to do with the school as far as Jimmy was concerned, and that was the way he wanted it. Every so often Jimmy would get into some kind of trouble but he'd take care of it himself; I never really knew the full details of what went on. One afternoon the principal of the high school called me at work and asked me to come right over because Jimmy had gotten into a fistfight with a teacher, a man. But then Jimmy got on the phone and said, "Don't come, Ma, I can handle it." He turned to the principal and yelled, "How dare you call my mother? She has no husband. She's at work. She has to work and take care of her children without anyone's help and you have the nerve to want her to come to school! This is my business, my problem. You deal with me, not her." I listened to all of this over the phone, and that was the last I knew of the incident. If Jimmy got into any scrapes I seldom heard about it. My cousin Natalie, whose daughter was the same age as Jimmy, would say to me, "What a bad boy he is. Why don't you do something about him?" But I didn't see how I could really give Jimmy any advice—not that he wanted it, anyway—because I felt that my life so far had been such a failure. I didn't feel that I had any right to tell him what to do, so I would say to Natalie, "Yes, yes, I'll talk to Jimmy," and then do nothing about it. He would come home and bring me money for the house and take care of Molly, and I'd just say, good boy, good boy. And that was really how I felt about my son.

Jimmy graduated from high school and decided that he did not want to go to college, at least not right away. He went down to Florida to see Buck and the next thing I knew he was about to get on a freighter bound for Ecuador. He called me from the dock just prior to sailing to say goodbye. Buck was with him and he said,

"Don't worry, Peggy, he'll be fine." Then Jimmy got back on the phone and said, "Sure, Ma, I might even come back one of these days." Buck had gotten Jimmy a job as apprentice to the ship's carpenter on a German boat hauling phosphate around the world. He was really on his own now, and I was proud of him. He certainly could do no worse with his life, I thought, than I had.

As soon as Molly was old enough to take care of herself I gave her her own key to the house and she would let herself in after school. She began taking piano lessons when she was seven and would practice until I came home from work. She was a well-behaved child, very quiet and polite to everyone. My children were my greatest joy. Jimmy wrote me letters from Guayaquil, Port of Spain, Rotterdam, Cartagena, Tangier, Bremen, Hamburg and Panama. He finally settled in England, where he attended the University of London. Jimmy once sent me a postcard that said, "I'll bet you didn't know that there are beautiful paintings in the loo at Buckingham Palace."

My father moved to Florida to live with Buck and his new wife, Julia. The climate was good for him but Jack didn't really like it there; he missed working and the faster life in Chicago. Tampa, where Buck had a thriving construction business, was a boom town. There was lots of money to be made there but it was still a southern city, life was slower than up north. Julia was good to my dad but he wrote and said that he didn't really feel a part of the family. He asked about Jimmy in each letter, his Babe. Jack had several more heart attacks, and with every one he seemed to become more senile. He was in his eighties now and it was hard for him to take care of himself.

When he'd lived in Chicago on his own in the couple of years prior to moving to Tampa, my father still carried on in the same

120

old ways. He'd take his lady friends to the Pump Room and the Cape Cod Room and run up large bills that he couldn't always pay. Jack McCloud had good credit everywhere, he had charge accounts in these places; but he didn't have the money anymore, and Buck would have to bail him out. Echoing Rose, Buck would say, "Let him enjoy himself, Peggy, it doesn't matter."

I felt badly about how I'd treated Jack, that I hadn't been nicer to him. I'd always harbored a resentment toward him stemming from his treatment of my mother. I didn't feel that he'd treated Rose right, and I didn't realize until I was older how wrong I was to hold this against him. I didn't know the whole story, or refused to see it in the proper perspective. My father was a gentle, generous man, with a unique attitude toward life that I had not completely understood. My mother's illness complicated their relationship and without needing to I'd taken her side against him. Jack and I got along all right but I was not as loving a daughter as I might have been. I used to scold him for spilling crumbs from his sandwich on the couch, crazy things like that.

Buck took Jack with him to Cuba, to Jamaica and the Bahamas. He was making good money and wanted to show his father a good time before it was too late. When he was eighty-three, Jack had a bad fall, which broke his hip. Soon after that Buck and Julia put him in a nursing home in St. Petersburg. He wrote me long letters from the nursing home, all about the old days, consistently referring to Jimmy as Buck, finally making no distinction between them at all. I'd always felt sorry for my mother, having to stay in bed while my father was running around, and that made me act coldly toward him, which I regretted now. Jack did what he had to and I had no right to judge him the way I had. Jack McCloud was a gracious man, a gentleman, with many friends. He had a very close relationship with his son and grandson. I never once heard him speak badly of someone when not in their presence.

My father never finished the last letter he was writing to me from the nursing home. "Dear Peggy," it read, "Please come and take me away from this place. I want to go home to Chicago. I can't stand it here another . . . " And he never wrote any more. His kidneys had started to fail, and he died of uremic poisoning, not his heart or his gall bladder or his diabetes or any of the hundred things brought on by his high living. His kidneys failed him after the fall and he could not exercise or walk properly. After he heard the news, Jimmy wrote me from London: "Pops was the best friend I ever had, and he always will be."

$\mathbf{B}$uck was doing well in the construction business in Florida, building houses, and beginning a new family with Julia. They had a daughter, Polly, exactly one year to the day younger than Molly. Buck had a son, Carl, by his first wife, Laura Mae, who lived near him in Tampa. Carl was a tall, handsome, smart boy who had just graduated from the University of Illinois and was eager to learn the construction business.

When Buck went overseas during the war he left Laura Mae in Philadelphia, where I visited her, and in his absence she really took to drinking too much and running around with a fast, ritzy crowd. She spent an awful lot of money, more than Buck could afford. She wouldn't buy a pair of shoes unless she had them hand made. When he got back from Europe he found a drunken woman and a pile of debts. Laura Mae had stuck Carl away in a military school and hadn't seen him for months. Buck tried to straighten her up, paid the bills, and moved them to Williamsburg, Virginia, where he commanded the second largest ship building service in the world. Everything would have been fine except that Laura Mae had become an alcoholic; their marriage foundered.

After the war ended Buck decided to leave the Navy and go into business on his own. To do that he needed a stake so he took a job building roads for the government in Alaska. He dropped Laura Mae off in Chicago on his way west, told her to clean herself up, to get off the booze before he got back, and went to the Yukon and Alaska for a year. He wrote me some marvelous letters from up there, about having to sleep outdoors in his bag with blinders on to block out the midnight sun; and how the bears would steal his food even when he hung it high off the ground from the branch of a tree. It was back breaking work but Buck finished his contract and came back with ten thousand dollars and a serious case of pneumonia. I met him at the train station and drove him directly to the hospital, where he stayed for three weeks. He looked terrible. I didn't even recognize my own handsome brother.

Laura Mae was alternately on and off the wagon, and after Buck returned from the northwest territories they didn't get along well. They decided to separate legally. That's when Buck went to Los Angeles to learn the building business. He stayed out there for two years, working as a civil engineer for the city of Van Nuys, and running around with all the Hollywood starlets.

He told me about one girlfriend of his who would never see him before ten o'clock at night. When he asked her why, she said that her time was always taken between six and ten. After that, she was free, but she wouldn't tell him what she was committed to for those four hours every evening. Buck guessed that she was seeing another fellow and one night he showed up early, a little before ten, on purpose. Sure enough, just as Buck arrived, there was a man coming down the walk from her house. As they passed, the man said hello and stopped to introduce himself. "My name's Howard Hughes," he said. "About time we met." Buck gave his name, they shook hands, and Hughes got into a limousine that was waiting at the curb and drove off. "Why didn't you tell me you were seeing Howard Hughes?" Buck asked his girlfriend. "He doesn't want anyone to know," she said. Buck explained that Hughes had just introduced himself to him on the sidewalk outside. "Well, I guess that's the end of that," she said. "What do you mean?" Buck asked. "If he told you who he was then it's over with me. He wouldn't have done that if he meant to come back, at least not for a while. That's just the way he is," said the girl. "I ought to know. I was married to him once for two weeks."

When Buck came back to Chicago he opened an office on La Salle Street and started the McCloud Construction Company. He went into partnership with another fellow and began developing property north and west of the city. He and Laura Mae reconciled and bought a house and for a little while things were working out all right. Laura Mae, however, thought that Buck could make more money if he went to work for Arnold Bradford, a friend of theirs who owned a hotel chain. Bradford was a close friend of Buck's who had helped him out from time to time and asked Buck to work for him. My brother wanted to make it on his own, though, and turned Bradford down. This made Laura Mae furious and she started hitting the bottle again. She also started having an affair with Arnold Bradford, who had recently divorced his wife. Buck suspected that something was going on, but said nothing to Laura Mae.

One day Buck said to me, "Would you like to go up to Lake Geneva on the weekend with Jimmy and Carl? I'll drive you up and rent a room at a lodge and you can have some fun with the boys boating and swimming. I'll leave you there and come back the next day. I have a little chore to perform in Chicago." I agreed to stay with the boys while he and a detective followed Laura Mae that weekend. Buck told her that he was taking the boys fishing, picked us up, and drove to Lake Geneva, where he left us, saying, "See you tomorrow." The boys, of course, knew nothing about what was going on.

Buck went back to town, met up with the detective, and that evening they saw Arnold Bradford's car come to pick up Laura Mae. They followed Bradford and Laura Mae to a hotel Bradford owned in Evanston, and at the proper moment Buck broke in on them. There was a big fight, and Buck knocked Bradford down, saying to him, "Arnold, you're my friend, my good friend. How could you do this?" I feel that Buck really did love Laura Mae.

They had their problems, but he was extremely upset and disappointed about the whole thing. Buck and Bradford had been real buddies, too. They used to go to the Chicago Athletic Club together and throw birthday parties for one another.

Before Buck began divorce proceedings, Laura Mae attempted suicide by swallowing sleeping pills. Carl found her passed out on the floor and called Buck, who raced over and got her to the hospital in time to save her. After the doctors had pumped her stomach and she revived, Laura Mae threatened Buck that if he divorced her she would do it again. She may have for all I know, but he divorced her anyway. Six months or so after the divorce was final, Laura Mae married Arnold Bradford; and one year later Bradford had a massive heart attack and died, leaving all of his money to Laura Mae.

She moved to Miami where she rented the penthouse of the Old Alabama Hotel and proceeded to spend Bradford's money as fast as she could. Laura Mae became a terrible alcoholic. I saw her several times over the next ten years and was horrified by her disintegration. When I stayed with her in Philadelphia she would get up in the morning and put a teaspoonful of sugar in a glass, fill it to the top with gin and drink it down as if it were orange juice.

The last time I saw Laura Mae, in Miami, she was lying in bed at noon with a case of gin beside her, drinking straight from the bottle. She had lost her teeth, her perfect, beautiful white smile, and had only the vaguest notion of who I was. I reminded her of the time she had taken me down to the beauty parlor in the Ambassador Hotel in Chicago and had my hair bleached blonde. I'd been wearing a blue polka-dot dress Laura Mae had given me and when I walked down the street all of the truck drivers whistled and hooted. When she and I came into my house my mother fainted at the sight of me; and when she came to Rose swore she would not let me stay the night in her house until I'd had the blonde taken out of my hair. I tried, that last time I saw her, to get Laura Mae to recall this and other events, but she was too far gone.

About a month later Laura Mae went out the penthouse window naked and broke her neck on Collins Avenue. Nobody had been found in her apartment and the cause of death was reported as accidental.

Buck took Carl to live with him and eventually met a nice, quiet girl named Julia Kavanagh, the daughter of another builder around Chicago. Julia was as different from Laura Mae as she could possbily be. Short, dark-haired and petite, Julia was kind, patient and crazy about Buck. I was very pleased when Buck asked her to marry him. She was just what he needed and I told him it was the smartest thing he'd ever done.

Their wedding party was held at a restaurant owned by an old friend of Rudy's, a mob guy named Bobby Domino whom I hadn't seen in years. "So tell me, Peggy," he said at the party, "how can you look even better now than you did fifteen years ago? Must be that quiet, uneventful life you've been living, huh?" "That must be it, Bobby," I said. "Yeah, the old days are gone," he said. "Sometimes it's hard to believe, but things will never be the same. Life's tough to figure, Peg. Just remember, never play all your chips on one number and you'll be a survivor." I was learning, I told Bobby, about what it takes to survive.

I remember when Jimmy was a little boy, after I had divorced Rudy, and even before, when we had the house in Miami, I'd say to him, "Come on, Jim, we're going down to Florida," or, "Let's go visit so-and-so in Atlanta. Hop in the car!" Jimmy would say, "Okay, Mom," and away we'd go. We had the best times together. He was a good little traveller and I was full of piss and vinegar in those days, I was always ready to go.

One night on our way to meet a fellow I knew in Jackson, Mississippi, we stopped up in the mountains in Chattanooga, Tennessee, at a motel on Lookout Mountain. It was very cold, the middle of the winter, and I had to get up during the night. I turned on the bathroom light and screamed. There were a hundred or more scorpions milling around on the floor, scorpions and cockroaches and huge centipedes. It was about three or four in the morning but I woke Jimmy up and said, "Let's go, kid. We're not staying here any longer." We grabbed our things and jumped in the car. Jimmy was a good sport, he never complained about anything when we were on the road.

We'd stop along the way at reptile farms, like the big one in St. Augustine, Florida, and look at the crocs and gators and snakes. I enjoyed this as much as Jimmy did. In Louisiana, near Bogalusa, we stopped at a place called "Elwood & Rooney's Home of the Dinosaurs." The dinosaurs turned out to be two half-dead iguanas, and Jimmy was irate. He was only seven years old but he demanded our fifty cents back and got it. We climbed back in the car and had a good laugh. He was the best kid! Jimmy was afraid of nothing, and when we were alone together on the road like that neither was I. It was the rest of the time that I caved in to the pressure other people put on me.

I was young when I had Jimmy, and I was young for my age. I'd been in Texas and New York for a while but I didn't really know anything. All that Kozeny and Rudy and the other men I knew were interested in was that I looked good and smiled a lot. When I was with Jimmy, alone and free, I could let go, enjoy myself and act however I chose to act. Jimmy was always proud of how I looked. Even later, when he was in high school, his boy friends would come over and say to him, "Is that your mother?" It was funny, and I guess it gave Jimmy a charge. That was when I had my looks. It's too bad my life wasn't settled in those early years, so that Jimmy could have had a more normal existence. I could have enjoyed things more, and done more for him.

I had all sorts of boyfriends and romances but they never meant anything real to me. I became careless with them. I was only interested in what they could do for me, and I didn't really care about that. If they gave me nice presents I liked them, or acted as if I did. The marriage to Mickey made me very bitter, and this was on top of the disappointment and resentment I carried with me from my time with Rudy. It was bitterness heaped on bitterness, and I developed a cruel streak in me after Mickey. After a while this wore off but I was determined to get away from this glamor girl image and the kind of lifestyle that went with it; that's one of the reasons I married a plain fellow like Andy.

After my divorce from Andy, while I was seeing Lee Randolph—though Lee was in L.A. or New York or Europe so often that I had lots of time in between—a suitor from my early days, Bob Crown, came back into the picture. Bob was originally from Montana and he was a championship polo player. I went many times to see him play at Oak Brook and we always got along well. Bob had a younger brother, Dick, who was a cripple and had been confined to a wheelchair since he was a young boy. Dick was a nice man, he was very bright, but he depended totally on his older brother; he needed constant care and Bob supported him. They had a sister back in Montana who was willing to have Dick live with her, but Dick loved Bob and wanted to be with him, so that's the way it was.

When Jimmy was a little boy Bob had a small polo mallet made for him, a replica of his own. He and Jimmy would play in front of our house on the lawn knocking the hard white polo balls around, pretending to be on horseback. Bob did like Jimmy and took him out to the polo field and held him up on his horse while he galloped from one end of the grounds to the other. Rudy sent Jimmy to cowboy camp up in Wisconsin a couple years later where Jimmy became the youngest horseman in the elite Night-hawks trail patrol. He always gave the credit for his interest and early skill in horseback riding to Bob Crown. In fact, Jimmy still has the little polo mallet Bob gave him thirty years ago.

By the time Bob came back into my life he had undergone several disappointments himself. He'd wanted to marry me after my divorce from Rudy but I didn't want to get married then, and Bob had gone off to other romances that had not worked out. He never had a lot of money. Bob earned his living by taking care of other people's horses. He had his brother Dick to care for, and I guess he never could marry the girls he wanted to marry. There had been a change in Bob, he was often depressed but never unkind. I began to think that I should really give him a chance, that maybe I should get married again. I was very fond of Bob but I didn't love him, so I demurred, thinking that perhaps something would happen and I'd feel more strongly about him as time went on. But it never got that far. Bob fell ill and died a miserable death. He developed a brain tumor that caused him to become insane; it just happened and there was nothing anyone could do about it. Bob was put into a hospital asylum and Dick went to Montana to live with their sister. Bob was not in the asylum for very long, six months at the most. I went to see him once but he couldn't talk or even look at me, it was horrible. And that was the end of Bob Crown.

I visited Buck from time to time at his home in Florida. His construction business had its ups and downs over the years, but he was able to make a good living. Julia became an avid bridge player and their daughter Polly developed into a champion swimmer. Molly and Polly, the two cousins, became good friends. Not only was their birthday the same, but they looked like twins. Though Molly was a year older, they were approximately the same height; even their voices were similar.

Jimmy lived in London for three years, going to school part of the time and working at a variety of jobs. He wrote regularly, telling me about his life there, and the interesting people he knew, like the fellow who had assassinated the King of Saudi Arabia in 1953 and now ran a coffee house in South Kensington. Then Jimmy met a Belgian girl and went with her to live in Paris. Occasionally he would ship out again, when he needed money, I suppose. Jimmy sent me gifts from Yokohama, Hong Kong and Dakar. He was living the kind of adventurous life I had always dreamed about, and I was happy for him. I worried about him but he was doing what he wanted to do and I knew that he could take care of himself. Jimmy was like Buck, he had an independent mind and didn't kowtow to anyone. He once told me he was glad in a way that Rudy had died before he could have the opportunity to try to steer Jimmy into any particular direction. Jimmy liked the idea of beginning his adult life on his own, with no one telling him what to do. I understood what he meant.

Meanwhile, my cousin Natalie wanted to introduce me to another fellow. I said no. After Andy Golden, I didn't want to meet any more men through her. But she insisted, telling me that this person was different, and that he wasn't the marrying type. He was just a guy to go out and have some fun with, she said, so I agreed to meet him. Armand Gary was an automobile dealer, he owned three or four Cadillac agencies in the Chicago area and was quite well-to-do. His father had owned the garage on the North side in which the St. Valentine's Day Massacre had taken place and the family, according to Natalie, was still "connected."

I found Armand to be a charming, nice-looking forty year old man. The only thing especially different about him was that he was stone deaf. He had lost his hearing at the age of four due to an infection and had no hope of ever regaining it. The loss of hearing did nothing to discourage Armand from making a fortune and living a full life. He read lips perfectly and reacted to sounds, vibrations, so that despite his handicap he was a marvelous dancer. Armand's timing on the dance floor was perfect, he had perfect rhythm; all his partner had to do was guide him in the proper direction. He had lots of girlfriends, many of whom wanted to marry him, but Armand, like Sam Stetson, preferred the bachelor life. He spoke well, if a trifle nasally, and he could speak on the telephone with the aid of a special device attached to the receivers at his home and office. If he called from another location he would have someone else do the talking and answering for him. As I say, it was not much of a handicap for Armand. He did tell me never to talk behind his back where he could not see my lips move; he liked to know what people around him were saying.

Armand had been married once, when he was much younger, and it hadn't worked out. Armand had dedicated himself, as he told me, to taking care of his parents and an older, spinster sister, and to making a lot of money. We became good friends. On

133

Sundays I would help him prepare and serve large brunches for his family and friends at his home in Winnetka, a suburb north of Chicago. Armand took me out to the best places, we had some wonderful dates. He knew about my ongoing relationship with Lee Randolph, but that didn't bother Armand at all; he had his other girls and I didn't mind that, either. We had what I believe was a totally honest relationship. I admitted to Armand that all my life I had envied my brother, especially in his younger days when he could do whatever he wanted, go anywhere, take out this girl and that one. But I was unable to do this because I was a girl. I was expected to wait for invitations, to stay home and be good. I really wanted to be a licentious old man and have my choice of gals—to love 'em and leave 'em, like Jack and Buck had done and Jimmy now was doing.

So Armand and I got along very well for a year or so. He once told me that he did not want me to go out with anyone he introduced me to; he didn't want me to see his friends on my own. "Then what are you introducing me to them for?" I asked him. "You don't want to get married." He didn't say anything about it to me after that, but I respected his wishes anyway. Armand was good to me, he was a nice fellow, but before too long I realized that I did not want to work forever, that Molly needed a real father, and that I was getting older. I needed security and companionship. Andy was undependable as far as his child support payments were concerned and he rarely had time for Molly. Lee and Armand were fine to see whenever I did see them, they were wonderful to me and generous to Molly; but their participation in my life only went so far and then stopped. I found that I still craved that seemingly impossible dream: the happy little home with a father, mother and child all cozy and secure in their heads and beds. If this truly was a fantasy on my part I was willing to accept it as one; but, I decided, I had to give it one more try.

Molly spent the summer prior to her eighth birthday in Florida with Buck and Julia and Polly. Just before she was due to return to me in Chicago, Molly came down with a respiratory virus and had to be hospitalized in Tampa. I was working and Buck told me to stay home, not to fly down, that he'd make sure she was properly taken care of. For several days Molly ran a high fever and when she arrived in Chicago two weeks later I could see that she'd lost a great deal of weight. Her respiratory infection was still active and I took her immediately to see Dr. Edgewood. Molly wasn't eating and she began to get severe nosebleeds at night. She had to stay in bed for a month but finally, thanks to constant care from Marcus, Molly recovered.

He suggested that I take her away for a few days to a vacation spot to help get her back on her feet before school started. I wasn't sure where to go; the only places I'd gone to on holidays were in Mexico, South America, Hawaii, Cuba or Florida. I didn't really know any resorts that were close by. Another doctor at the hospital suggested a place called Deer Run Lodge in Wisconsin, just outside of Madison. In fact, he said, he and his wife were going up there on the coming weekend and would look in on us to see how we were doing. It sounded good to me. The lodge was only four hours from Chicago and it had ponies, swimming and train rides for children. I took a short leave of absence from the hospital, packed enough clothes for about ten days and drove up to Deer Run with Molly.

The lodge was a lovely little hideaway. I made sure that Molly took it easy for a couple of days and didn't run around too much. She enjoyed herself tremendously, playing on the swings and splashing in the pool. I relaxed, slept late, read and wrote letters to Jimmy and Buck. Jimmy was in California. He'd gotten paid off a ship in San Pedro and gone up to the coast to San Francisco, where he'd decided to stay for a while. I wanted to see him and wrote asking him to come to Chicago for Thanksgiving.

On the weekend my doctor friend and his wife arrived and we all went out to dinner. They asked me if I would like to meet a friend of theirs from Madison, a man in his early forties named Jake LaPointe. Jake was in the trucking business, they said, he was divorced and the father of two children; perhaps we could all go out together the next night. I said that I would be glad to accompany them provided I could find a sitter for Molly. We agreed to talk again in the morning.

As it turned out, Jake LaPointe already had a date for the next night, but my friends insisted that I come along with them anyway. We would be dining at the same restaurant as Jake and his date and they would introduce me to him. I got one of the hotel maids to stay with Molly and we drove into Madison. We went to a very busy place, a restaurant with a long bar, and in the middle of it, at the largest table, I saw a young-looking, dashing fellow with black, wavy hair and brilliant smile surrounded by a flock of pretty girls. "There's Jake!" my doctor friend said, pointing to the man in the center table. He and Jake waved to each other and we were seated at a table across the room.

Jake came over, said hello to my friends, and they introduced us. He sat and talked with us for a few minutes, then excused himself and went over to the bar where he was greeted affectionately by a young woman. He stayed there for a bit then went over and talked with some other people. Jake was zooming around from table to bar to table. I thought to myself, "What a popular fellow." He was dressed very well, in a sharp blue suit, and everyone he spoke to seemed glad to see him. One of the women with whom he'd been sitting came over to our table and said hello to the doctor—they were friends of hers, too—and she sat down with us.

Her name was Nancy and she had apparently been a girlfriend of Jake's off and on for a number of years. She started talking to me about him. "I only wish I could pin him down," she said. "Look at him there, running from table to table; he's got more girlfriends that you can shake a stick at. I've been trying to get him to marry me for forever." I told her to be patient and let Jake have his flings, maybe he'd come back to her. I was trying to console her but not too seriously. I didn't know her or Mr. LaPointe, and I just sort of laughed at the whole thing. Nancy seemed to have had one drink too many and was obviously feeling down. She had five children, she said; she was divorced but she had a lot of money and owned a fancy dress shop in Madison.

Nancy talked about her children, to me and to the doctor's wife, but I tuned out of the conversation. I'd never been interested in small talk and gossip about children and what you were making for dinner. I liked to cook and keep house, I knew how to do those things and in fact took great pride in my abilities in those areas, but the time I had spent as a housewife with Andy had really bored me. Perhaps if he had been the right guy and I had been more in love and proud of him I would have been satisfied, but it didn't work out that way. I was happier when I was working, learning new things and meeting interesting people. I suppose I wanted things both ways. I was still confused about what I wanted, what I should be doing. I saw the dilemma as being mine alone, however; I didn't realize that other women felt similar frustrations. I was past forty and as unsure of myself as ever.

The next day Jake LaPointe called me at the Deer Run Lodge. He was very polite. He told me how glad he was to have met me, that he was sorry he'd already had a date for the previous evening but that he would be very pleased if my daughter and I would have dinner with him that night. Jake said he wanted to take us to a nice place quite nearby the lodge where a friend of his was singing and where they had a good orchestra. Did I like to dance? he asked. I said yes, and we agreed on a time for him to pick us up.

Molly was feeling good again. She'd had a fine day riding horses and swimming and the color had returned to her face. She was excited about going out to dinner and she said to me, "I have a feeling, mother, that Mr. LaPointe won't have a Cadillac like all of your other boyfriends. I think he'll have an old car." Molly was half right: Jake arrived in a new station wagon. He was delighted to meet Molly; he thought she was the most gorgeous and well-behaved little girl he'd ever seen. She took to him immediately, too, which surprised me. Andy had not been much of a father to her, she didn't really know what it was to have a man pay her proper paternal attention. Molly opened up to Jake like I'd never seen her do with a man before, talking a mile a minute. They hugged one another and he took her out on the dance floor and waltzed her around. Jake introduced her to his friend, the singer, and she dedicated the next song to Molly. Jake ordered Molly everything on the menu that she wanted. It really was Molly's big night on the town and she thought Jake was the greatest.

The three of us had a wonderful evening. Jake was a good dancer, the band was terrific, and we had fun doing all kinds of different dance steps. By the end of the evening Molly was exhausted and Jake had to carry her up the stairs to our room. While I put her to bed Jake waited for me on the hotel porch. I went back down and sat with him, talking until three in the morning.

Jake told me how he had broken away from the family business, LaPointe Steel, to start his own hauling company. He owned a dozen trucks that transported goods, mostly heavy equipment, throughout the Midwest. His family had been pioneers in the area, having come from France to America in the eighteenth century. Jake admitted that he was something of a black sheep in the family. After the death of his father he'd disagreed with his brothers about how the business should be run and they'd had a serious falling out. Their mother had been dead for many years and Jake rarely saw his brothers or other relatives now.

Jake had married his high school sweetheart, had two children with her, and they'd divorced after only four and a half years together. She had remarried and moved to Ohio; the children, a boy and a girl, lived with her. Jake hadn't seen them in five years. The daughter had spent some time in various homes for wayward girls and his son, who called Jake on the phone every six months or so, wanted to join the Marines as soon as he was old enough. Jake said that he sent them money whenever they asked for it, but he didn't really know who they were. "I blew it with them, Peggy," he said. "I never knew my kids. That's why I like Molly so much. I never had the opportunity to raise a child, to be close to my kids when they were growing up. It's my greatest regret."

I told Jake about my marriages, that I'd had a rough go of it, in different ways, with each one. Rudy had been a domineering man, I said, but a good one. He never lied to me, never; but he never gave me a chance to be myself. Mickey didn't really count; his mental problems obviated any opportunity we might have had to make a marriage work. My marriage to Andy had been a very unfortunate one, I explained. Molly really had no father to speak of; Andy didn't even think enough of her to send the few bucks each week that he was supposed to. I'd stopped bugging him about it, I told Jake, it wasn't worth the aggravation. I was able to support Molly and myself with my job at the hospital. I was extremely reluctant to allow myself to depend on anyone again.

Jake talked for hours about his life, about his childhood in Deer Run—he'd grown up in a house not even two miles from where we were sitting—and his college days at the University of Wisconsin, where he'd played on the football team. He'd been a Navy pilot during the Korean War and had seen quite a bit of action. Until recently, Jake told me, he'd flown his own plane. His eyes weren't as good as they used to be, he said, so he'd had to give it up. Jake was a great talker, a crackerjack salesman, and he was doing a wonderful job of selling himself to me. I felt great compassion for him. I admired his ambition and ability to build a business without any help from anybody else. He told me that he was a year older than me, though he really was a year younger. Later when I asked him about why he'd done that he said that he thought I'd like him better if he were older than I was.

We sat on the porch and traded stories until I got so tired that I just had to go up to bed. Here I'd thought, after seeing him in action at the restaurant the night before, that he was a fast guy, a blade; but Jake was a sweetheart and a perfect gentleman. He told me that he wanted to take me out again the next evening but I said that Molly and I had to go back to Chicago; she had to start school in two days. We kissed good night and he drove off. The next morning he called and asked if he could take Molly and me to breakfast before we left. I said that sounded fine and Jake came right over in his station wagon; he'd stopped on the way and bought flowers for me and a doll for Molly. I'd never met such a thoughtful man before. We had breakfast and I gave him my home phone number. Jake promised to call very soon and wished us a safe journey, kissed Molly and gave me a hug. I drove off in a kind of daze, wondering just who Jake LaPointe really was.

J ake called sooner than I thought he would. As Molly and I stepped into the house in Chicago the phone was ringing. "Did you have a good trip home?" he asked. "I miss you already. I'm going to come in as soon as I can to see you." For the first time in quite a while I was utterly intrigued and fascinated by a man. Jake LaPointe was from out of town, he was young and full of pep. As much as I liked Lee Randolph I wanted to be with somebody my own age, and someone who was eligible for a change. Jake had a good background, a college education, and he'd built his own business from scratch. I was impressed by that as well as by his rapport with Molly. The next afternoon Jake called me at work to say hello and to make a date for the following Sunday; he'd be at my house for breakfast at eleven.

I prepared the table carefully for Jake's arrival and Molly got all dressed up. It was a bright, sunny Sunday and I thought that perhaps after eating we could all go to the park. By noon, however, Jake had still not arrived; nor had he called. At one o'clock I put everything away and took Molly to the park by myself. I was more upset by Jake's not showing up than I had thought it possible for me to be; after all, I reasoned with myself, I hardly knew him. What difference did it make? But Molly had been very disappointed and that disturbed me. It was one thing to stand me up but quite another to do this to a child.

By six that evening I was prepared to forget all about Jake

LaPointe; then he called. "I'm very sorry, Peg," he said. "One of my drivers had some trouble and I had to drive all the way to Des Moines to take care of it." I asked him why he hadn't called earlier. "I didn't want to wake you at seven, when I had to leave my house," he said. "And I did try later but there was no answer." Yes, I told him, Molly and I had gone out in the afternoon. "Give me another chance, Peggy," Jake said. "Let's try it again next Sunday. I promise to be there no matter what happens." I said all right, next week then, and he sounded relieved and very happy. He asked to speak to Molly so I put her on the phone and she giggled and laughed at whatever he was saying before throwing Jake a kiss and hanging up. Naturally all of this was piquing my interest.

The next Sunday Jake arrived an hour late. He looked bad, as if he had been up very late the night before. For the first time I noticed how deeply lined his face was, too wrinkled for a man his age. He was smoking a lot and asked for a shot of scotch with his breakfast. I asked him if he felt all right and he said yes, he was fine, and he perked up. I figured he'd been running around till late with one of his girls up in Madison, drunk too much and needed to rest. I suggested to Jake that he take a nap in the back room of the house, Jimmy's old room, where he wouldn't be disturbed; but he insisted that he was okay, just a little tired. We had brunch and Jake stayed the day, talking with me and playing with Molly. About six we all went out for a Chinese dinner. Jake was as polite and considerate as he had been in Deer Run, and we enjoyed ourselves tremendously. At dinner Jake and I held hands and when he said goodbye he kissed me on the cheek. It was like an old-fashioned courtship.

That night before I went to sleep I took my grandpa Boris's gold pocket watch out of the top drawer of the table next to my bed. I always kept his watch there because I liked to look at if often; it reminded me of him and my grandmother, Eva. I thought about grandpa Boris with his big red mustache, his old gray sweater worn over a crisp white shirt with the high, stiff collar. He always wore immaculately shined, black lace up shoes, and he'd sit and read the paper every night with his legs crossed in a high-backed, walnut rockingchair. He was a lovely man, never rude to his family. I loved to ask him what time it was because then he would take his beatiful gold watch, the chain of which was draped across his sweater, out of a little side pocket, and flick open the compartments. He always kept his wife Eva's picture in one side of the watch. Grandpa Boris would tell me the time but before he could replace the watch in his pocket I'd ask him to show me. The hands resembled intricately formed golden lanterns hung on the ends of poles; they obliterated the Roman numerals as they passed over them. I liked to look at the photograph of my grandmother, taken in Constantinople when she was twenty years old. She had such beautiful long black hair then, which she always wore pinned up. Of course by the time I knew Eva her hair was gray, and I never saw her with it down.

I looked at Boris's watch, at the picture of my grandmother, and thought about Jimmy, to whom I wanted to give it. I had tried to give it to him when he graduated from high school but Jimmy had said for me to keep it for him. He knew how much the watch meant to me and he was afraid, he said, that something might happen to it if he took it just then. "I'll take it later, Ma," he said, "when I'm settled down. You take care of it for me."

I hoped that Jake LaPointe was a good man, an honest man. I was frightened by the thought of making another mistake. I wanted Molly to have a good life, not to suffer, like Jimmy had, as a result of my poor judgment. I wanted everything from now on to go well, and I kissed grandpa Boris's watch for luck.

Jake started calling me every day at work. The other women at the hospital knew I was eager to receive his calls, so if I was away from my desk when he telephoned they made sure to have me paged. I was flattered by Jake's frequent phone calls and the flowers he had sent to me following his first Sunday visit. I encouraged his courtship but at the same time I had other friends and dates. Being four hours away by car it was not easy for Jake to see me very often.

I met a man named Henry Short who came to the hospital to visit a patient. Henry was an older man, in his late fifties, who owned a building supply company. He asked me out to lunch one day and I accepted, having nothing more in mind than that it would be a friendly daytime date, nothing serious. Henry, however, had other ideas. He told me that his wife of many years had recently died; he did not like living alone and wanted to remarry. Henry was not particularly attractive, but he was a nice guy, financially set, and he kept after me to go out with him for dinner. I wasn't sure that I wanted to do this so I put him off. He invited me to his house, with Molly, for a Sunday afternoon lunch with his children, two daughters, both of whom were married. I went by for lunch, met his daughters, who were very nice, and decided that Henry was a decent, sincere fellow. I had to give him a chance, too.

I agreed to go out to dinner and a nightclub with Henry and one of his daughters and her husband. We were at the club when his son-in-law happened to mention to me that Henry had been married very briefly just after his wife's death. I asked Henry about this and he said, "Oh, she was a crazy kid. Too young for me. I was a fool. I gave her the sun and the moon. She stole a big diamond ring from me. I couldn't wait until I had it annulled." I didn't like the fact that he had not told me about this marriage, but I let it go. Henry obviously was uncomfortable talking about it.

While Henry and I were dancing I noticed a young woman I knew who had been a friend of Buck's dancing with a fellow across the room. Katy Calloway had dated Buck before he met Julia and she and I waved to each other. She came over to me and said hello, introducing her partner. I turned to introduce Henry but he was gone, he'd run back to the table. I didn't understand why he'd taken off but I told Katy to come over and visit with us. She said she'd be glad to as soon as this dance was over. I sat down with Henry and a few minutes later Katy and her date came by. She said hello but took one look at Henry and excused herself.

I didn't understand what was going on. Henry wouldn't say anything, so I went over to Katy's table and asked her what was wrong. "I just divorced that horrible man," she said. "What horrible man?" I asked. "Henry Short, the man you're with." What a coincidence! I liked Katy, she was still friends with Buck, and I knew there was nothing crazy about her. She was a young, beautiful, intelligent girl about whom I'd heard only the best things. I told her that Henry had said she'd stolen a big diamond ring from him and Katy said, "Are you kidding? I gave him back everything he'd given me. I knew I'd made a mistake a week after I'd married him." "How could you marry him in the first place?" I asked her. "He's thirty years older than you." "Well," she said, "he seemed so nice and really wanted me to marry him. He's quite well off, too. But he was like an old lady, a complaining, nagging old lady. And he snored so loudly that I had to sleep on the other side of the house. I nearly had a nervous breakdown." Katy laughed. "He's the crazy one, not I."

145

I rejoined Henry and his daughter and said, "I've known Katy Calloway for several years, she used to go out with my brother. She's a swell girl." I told Henry that I didn't like lies, that he should have told me about this marriage. I left the club by myself and took a cab home. I had a bad taste in my mouth about the whole thing and didn't want anything further to do with Henry Short. A year later I heard that he was running around with the ex-wife of a mobster I'd met with Rudy what seemed like a hundred years before. This episode with Henry disturbed me and I told Jake about it. "You've got to be honest with me," I said to him. "I'm tired of lies, I've had it with dishonest men." "Don't worry, Peggy," Jake told me, "one thing I'll never do is lie to you."

Jake came to Chicago to see me on three or four occasions—he was never late again, or if he thought he might be he made certain to telephone—and then invited Molly and me to visit him at his home in Deer Run. Deer Run was a picturesque little town, full of large, old white wood houses with smoke coming out of the chimneys. To get to Jake's house, following his instructions, Molly and I drove across rickety wooden railroad bridges, down neat, narrow, well-kept streets. It was the kind of town I'd always fantasized myself living in, a Middle-American storybook land. On the day Molly and I drove up to see Jake the sky was full of snow, it shimmered in the early afternoon light. I liked the crisp, cold air and the smell of woodsmoke that greeted us as we got out of the car on Nelson Lane, in front of the old LaPointe family home where Jake still lived.

Jake's house had been built by his grandfather. It was a sixteen room, two-story wooden structure, with a screened-in porch that ran around one side of the house from front to back. Old Man LaPointe, as everyone in the town had called Jake's grandfather, had been a prize rose grower, and Jake's brother, Joseph, still paid for a gardener to tend the rose beds. In fact, Nelson Lane had been dubbed "Rose Alley" by the local residents because of Old Man LaPointe's dedication to his garden; the old timers around there still called it that. I fell in love with the house, the little street, the entire setting. It reminded me of my family's house in Prairie Park

147

and I thought about my dog, Toy, rolling in the snow in the front yard. I longed for that kind of peaceful haven again; for Molly, especially. I didn't like the city anymore, it was becoming too dirty, and the neighborhood we lived in was changing. Many of the long time residents were dying off or selling their homes now that their children had grown up and moved away. I could easily imagine myself living in the semi-rural environment of Deer Run, Wisconsin.

Jake welcomed us warmly. Once inside I was surprised to find the house sparsely furnished, though what furniture there was pleased me. I asked Jake about this and he said that his brothers' wives had cleaned the place out for their own homes, leaving him only the bare minimum. He lived alone; his brothers had agreed to let him occupy the house before it was sold. "You shouldn't sell this beautiful place," I told him. "I have to, Peggy," Jake said. "That was part of my agreement with my brothers. I want to buy a new house, on the other side of town. New factories are being built just up the street, anyway. The neighborhood is going to change and it won't be the same around here."

Jake explained that he'd been in business for himself for only two years. It had been difficult for him to get started after leaving LaPointe Steel, but now he was on his feet. "I'm starting a new life, Peg," Jake said. "I feel like I might be, too," I told him, almost before I knew what I was saying. We smiled at one another and then he took Molly's hand and proceeded to show us around the property.

I was enchanted with Jake. He was a sweet fellow, not a wolf. He was gentle and kind to Molly and considerate and gentlemanly with me. Jake was eager for us to see all of the country around Deer Run, so that afternoon we took a long ride, looking at everything, with Jake acting as tour guide. The town was surrounded by farmland and Jake took us down backroads and showed us lakes and streams we hadn't seen when we were there during the summer. The countryside was beautiful and I was very excited at the prospect of beginning a new life there. I knew I was getting ahead of myself a bit in my thinking but I began to consider the idea of moving to Deer Run even if things did not work out between Jake and myself. That evening Jake took us to a fine restaurant near Madison and again Molly had a ball, Jake allowing her to order everything on the menu that she wanted.

Jake insisted that Molly and I spend the night at his house. It was a four hour drive to Chicago and I gladly accepted his offer. He had already fixed up a bedroom for us and Molly fell asleep as soon as her head hit the pillow. Jake and I stayed up late in front of the fireplace in the living room, talking as we had on our first date. He became very serious and said that he wanted to marry me. His first marriage, Jake said, had been an unhappy one. He knew the mistakes that he'd made and he wouldn't repeat them. I told him again how wary I was of trusting a man; if I remarried it would be for the last time. Jake said that he understood how I felt, and he did not want to rush me into a decision. We agreed to wait for a while and see how things went. After all, we had not known each other very long. I kissed Jake good night and crawled into bed with Molly.

That night I had a dream that I had moved away from Chicago and was living on a desert. Other houses were clustered around mine but surrounding them was a vast desert. I decided, in the dream, to go back to my old house in Chicago to visit. I said goodbye to my neighbors in the desert community and they all acted as if they were never going to see me again. Back in Chicago, on my old street, I realized that I had no key to the house in which I'd lived, so I couldn't get in. Next door to the house, on an empty lot—I don't know what happened to the house that had been there—there was a carnival in progress. I wandered into it and marveled at the colorful booths, the games, the clowns in the aisles, a gigantic ferris wheel. In a seat at the top of the ferris wheel was Molly; she was alone and waving gaily at me. I waved back and yelled, "What are you doing here? I didn't know you were here!" She didn't hear me, though, and just kept on waving. I saw a woman ahead of me in the crowd who looked like my mother,

149

but she quickly disappeared. Florence O'Malley, my former next door neighbor, appeared beside me and I said, "Florence, how are you? How is Harry"—her husband—"and how are the kids?" "Fine, Peg, fine," she said. "Have you seen Rose?" I asked her. "My mother. Is she here?" Florence nodded. "She's around here somewhere," she said. "I think she said Jack was getting out of the hospital soon."

The noise of the carnival was very loud and when I woke up in the morning I could still hear it. I lay in bed for several minutes before I got up, letting the noise and colors from my dream diminish. I couldn't remember ever having had such a vivid dream before, one that seemed so absolutely real. I could hear Molly laughing downstairs. I liked hearing her screamy little laugh. All of a sudden I missed my mother terribly and I started to cry. Oh Rose, I thought, why are you so far away?

Jake came to Chicago every weekend following my visit to Deer Run. At Thanksgiving Jimmy came in from San Francisco and I introduced him to Jake. They seemed to get along all right but after Jake left, when I asked Jimmy what he thought of him, Jimmy said, "Are you going to marry him?" I answered that I didn't know for sure yet, I was still thinking about it. "He's a nice guy," Jimmy said. "But he talks like a big shot. He tries too hard to make himself sound important. What do you know about him?" I told Jimmy about Molly's and my visit to Deer Run, and what Jake had told me about his business. I said that Jake was the nicest, most sincere man I'd met in many years. "I hope you're right, Ma," Jimmy said. "You don't have to get married for money, you know. Uncle Buck and I can help you out." I kissed Jimmy and hugged him. "I know," I said. "Thank you, but I'll be all right." "I'm sure he's okay, Ma," Jimmy said. "I just worry about you, that's all."

Jake and I got married on Christmas Day. I had to sell my house so I stayed in Chicago until I found a buyer. Meanwhile, Jake oversaw the sale of the LaPointe place and put a down payment on a new two-bedroom house on the outskirts of Deer Run. I introduced Jake to Dr. Edgewood, who was sorry to be losing me from my job at the hospital. Marcus was suspicious of Jake and asked him a lot of questions, which I thought Jake handled rather well. Marcus took me to lunch one day and, echoing Jimmy, said,

"What do you really know about this man, Peggy? Are you sure you're doing the right thing?" I told Marcus how kind Jake was, and how much Molly liked him. "A good way to get to the mother is through the child," Marcus said. "You're a fantastic woman, Peg. I hope LaPointe knows that, and that he's worthy of you." I thanked Dr. Edgewood for all he'd done for me and for his kind words. "Rose McCloud was a dear friend of mine," he said. "As long as I'm able to I'll help you in any way that I can." Two months after our conversation about Jake, Dr. Edgewood had a stroke and died. I moved into the new house in Deer Run the day after his funeral.

Jake showed me his warehouse and the garage where his trucks were housed. I knew he wasn't wealthy but his business was prospering and his reputation in the town seemed good. LaPointe Steel was a big local company and everyone knew the LaPointe brothers: Jake, Joseph and Bill. I met Joseph and Bill and their wives on separate occasions, each by accident. They were very cordial to me, but Jake said that he wanted nothing to do with them. He was bitter about how the family business had been divided up after their father's death and had no intention of socializing with his brothers. They still lived in the old part of town, near the steel company; the house Jake had bought for us was in a tract as far away as possible from Nelson Lane. There were new schools nearby for Molly to go to, and I was pleased by our little house. It was not as grand as the old LaPointe home but I was satisfied. Jake told me that he had taken nothing from the sale of the house, he let it all go to his brothers, and I believed him. I did not want to interfere in his dealing with his family, especially as I knew nothing—and still don't—of the details involved regarding the split. Jake refused to talk about it and I did not press him.

I had the money from the sale of my parents' house, and I sent half to Buck and invested my share in helping to furnish the new home in Deer Run. Buck wrote me that he would keep the money I'd sent him in a separate account for me; if ever I needed it, he said, it would be there. My house in Deer Run was not exactly the house I'd dreamed about but I felt that it was a start. I was glad to be out of the city and had no trouble making new friends in the town. As soon as spring came I dug up part of the yard and put in a garden. I planted flowers all over the place. I was enjoying myself tremendously and so was Molly.

Shortly after we were married and moved into the new house, Jake put a piece of paper in front of me and told me to sign it. I asked him what I was signing and he said, "Don't you dare ask me what it is. Just sign." This attitude shocked me; I'd never heard a harsh word from him before. I signed the paper, though, and said nothing. Later, he apologized for his manner and explained that it was nothing important, he'd needed a witness for something. He'd had a rough day, he said, and asked me to forgive him, which I did.

I was very much in love with Jake at this point. He was a good lover and he was sweet to Molly, but he had a ferocious male ego. He was the king, and I let it go. I believed in Jake and wanted this marriage to work so I began to capitulate in order to appease him. If he was in what appeared to be a bad mood I left him alone, and pretty soon he would come out of it and everything was all right. Jake didn't like to discuss his business with me and since I knew nothing about trucks or transportation of goods I stayed out of his affairs. He gave me enough money for groceries, for the household, and I had a little of my own in the bank so I wasn't worried. I knew Jake worked hard and I did my best to support him emotionally.

Molly began to have asthma attacks during our first summer in Deer Run and I took her to several doctors in order to help her. One of them recommended that I take her to see a specialist in Colorado and when I asked Jake for the money for a trip out there he told me he didn't have it, that I should use my own. He said that he was a little short right then, that he'd reimburse me as soon as he could. I withdrew money from my savings and drove to Denver with Molly. The doctor told me that the climate in Wisconsin was bad for her, that she should be living in the Southwest. As that was impossible, he prescribed treatment as best he could and we drove back home. Molly's asthma afflicted her, often severely, over the next several years. It was not until she moved to Arizona, when she was twenty, that the asthma abated.

Florence O'Malley came to visit me after I'd been married to Jake for a year. She and I were sitting in the kitchen talking when Jake came home for dinner. He barely said hello to us and walked into the bedroom and closed the door. A few minutes later he came out and sat down at the kitchen table, looked at Florence and said, "Can Peggy and Molly go back to Chicago with you? I've just lost everything. My business is gone and the sheriff is after me."

Florence and I were shocked. "What do you mean?" I asked. "Why is the sheriff after you?" "I owe a lot of money," Jake said. "I haven't paid my bills and they're closing my doors. They've impounded my trucks. It's over, Peg, I'm sorry. I'm no good. I thought I could make it but I can't." He put his head in his hands and cried. "How much do you need?" I asked him. "What will it take to get you out of debt?" He told me and I said, "Don't worry, Jake, I can have Buck send me the other half of the money I made on the sale of my house. You can use that." I comforted Jake and looked at Florence. She didn't know what to say. "Come on, Jake," I said, "we'll make it. You'll feel better after you've had dinner."

I gave Jake the balance of my house money and he settled his affairs. He got his trucks back and promised to pay me every cent I'd loaned him within a year. Jake insisted that the money I'd given him was a loan. I had to believe in him now, I told Jake, because I had nothing left. He assured me that he would not fail again, that I shouldn't doubt him. Molly and I meant the world to him, he said.

For a while things did get better. Jake seemed to be doing well, even speaking of expanding his business, buying more trucks, and I made some good friends, becoming quite active in civic affairs. My name was often in the local paper in connection with various clubs and organizations. I was changing, feeling part of the community and learning about things I never would have thought I'd be interested in like flower arranging, landscaping and painting. I enrolled in art classes at the Deer Run extension of the University of Wisconsin. We'd never had a honeymoon, and Jake began to talk about our getting away somewhere for a few weeks. I was sure that now everything would go well for us.

I was digging in the garden one morning when the phone rang. It was Jake. "I'm in jail, Peggy," he said. "They arrested me as soon as I got to work. They were waiting for me." I couldn't believe it. "Why?" I asked. "I thought you paid all your bills. What's this about?" "Call Barney Woods," Jake said, "he'll tell you." I'd never heard of Barney Woods. "Who's he?" I asked. "A lawyer," said Jake. "He's in the book, in Madison." Then he hung up. I just stood there with the receiver in my hand, staring at the calendar on the wall. I tried to think of what day of the week it was, what month, the year, but I couldn't. My eyes did not focus when I looked at the calendar. I wanted to cry but I couldn't. What now? I thought. Oh Jesus, what now?

Barney Woods was a tax lawyer. Jake had not filed an income tax return of any kind for fifteen years and the government had caught up with him. When tax time came around the first year we were married Jake told me to file by myself. When I said that that seemed foolish, that we would be losing money unless we filed together, Jake said, "Do what I tell you, Peg. I'm taking care of it separately." I did not argue, figuring that he knew what he was doing. Barney Woods told me that the tax people had been on to Jake for the last two years. Jake had promised to make some payments but he hadn't and now they'd arrested him for income tax evasion. Bail had been set at ten thousand dolllars.

I went to see Jake, who was being held in the Federal Building in Madison, and asked him what I should do. Should I sell his trucks? "No," he said, "all of my property's been attached." "What about our house?" I asked. "Can they take that?" "I put the house in Joseph's name," said Jake. "It belongs to him." "Joseph's name?" I said. "I thought you never spoke to Joseph!" "He did me a favor when we sold the family place; he put the down payment on our house." I asked Jake why he hadn't told me this before, why he hadn't told me about his tax problems. Why hadn't he paid his taxes in the first place? And for fifteen years! What else didn't I know about him that I should? Jake told me to go see Joseph about the bail, to not worry about him. "What do you mean not worry about you?" I said. "I'm worried about myself! And Molly."

Joseph LaPointe was a large, soft-spoken man. He was four years older than Jake and had never had any children. He told me that Jake had always been an impatient man, even as a kid he had to have things his own way and right now. Nobody had ever been able to tell Jake what to do or how to do it. The tax business did not surpise Joseph. Nothing Jake did surprised him, he said. I asked Joseph the reason for Jake's split from LaPointe Steel, why he refused to have anything to do with his family, but Joseph would not tell me. He would only say that Jake would be bailed out and everything would be taken care of, for me not to worry. "Not to worry!" I said. "That's what Jake told me. How can I not worry? I gave your brother my last cent and all either of you can say is not to worry!"

Jake came home the next day and went to sleep for sixteen hours. When he woke up I told him that I was going to get a job, that we would share the house payments and that I would take care of Molly. I'd called Jimmy the night before and had a long talk with him. I told him what had happened and he said, "You've got to stop letting other people run your life." It hadn't occurred to me before but he was right; all my life I'd deferred to other people, even when I thought I was in control. The problem was how to change once and for all. I loved Jake, I didn't want to let him down now that he was in trouble, but I had to do something positive for myself.

I did get a job, working in the billing department of an insurance office. It was full-time, five days a week. I made sure Molly got to school all right in the morning and went to the office. She let herself into the house after school, as she'd done when I'd worked at the hospital, and practiced the piano or did her homework. Joseph and Barney Woods worked out some kind of a deal for Jake with the Internal Revenue boys. Maybe Joseph paid Jake's debt, I don't know, nobody would tell me. Jake started up a new business, managing security forces for the large local corporations like Sunstrand and Wheeler Industries. He told me he was paying his income tax; still separately, however.

My health deteriorated during this period. I became very nervous and gained weight, too much weight. I'd never been fat in my life, even though I was tall and large-boned, but I was troubled and began to eat to pacify myself. My looks changed for the worse; I was frumpy and becoming another person physically. Old friends of mine from Chicago were upset when they saw me. My cousin Natalie, whom I saw at her mother's, my Aunt Lilia's funeral, was shocked by my appearance. She said she would not have recognized me on the street.

What was wrong with me? What was I doing wrong? I knew I had nobody but myself to blame for the turn my life had taken, but how could all three of the men I'd chosen to marry since Rudy had such runs of astounding bad luck? Rudy had been a good provider, a good man in his own way, but I was not sorry I had left him. I didn't want his kind of life. Things just hadn't worked out the way I would have liked with Rudy, but that was all right. I had Jimmy from that marriage and that was more than enough. But the others! How could my judgment have been so poor? To what in each of them had I blinded myself? I could not pinpoint the flaw in my own character that had caused me to saddle myself with such a succession of ignominious losers.

I fought to control my weight and tried to do my best around the house. I shared the household expenses with Jake, who was up and down in his security business. I'd ask him how it was going and one week he'd say, "Bad." I'd ask him the same thing the next week and he'd say, "Good." For the first time in years I had trouble with eczema; small eruptions appeared on my neck and under my arms.

I visited Buck in Tampa and asked him what I should do. Should I leave Jake? Buck couldn't tell me; it was up to me, he said. The thought of divorcing a fourth husband horrified me. I did not want to admit I'd made the wrong choice again. Jimmy

158

was working as a carpenter in California and he wrote that he would be glad to help me out, to give me money, but not so long as I was married to Jake. Jimmy was afraid I'd give it to him. He felt that it was Jake's responsibility as my husband to take care of me and Molly. If I divorced Jake, however, both Buck and Jimmy were willing to do what they could. I did not want to depend on my brother or my son. I kept my job at the insurance office, even though the pay was low, and tried to save some small amount each week.

I liked my friends in Deer Run. I was satisfied with my little house, my garden, my yard. I played golf with other ladies on the weekends, became a decent bridge player and stayed active socially, though on a modest level. I did my best to maintain a proper front, to keep up appearances even when Jake brought home no money for weeks at a time. Molly would go on the bus to Chicago every so often to see her father, and he started to send her support money on a fairly regular basis for the first time. When she was fifteen, Molly got a job working after school in the stockroom at a pharmacy near our house. Her asthma hampered her severely at times but she was stoic about it, knowing that, barring a move to a warm, dry climate, there was not much we could do.

I learned by accident, by reading some papers Jake had left on his dresser, that Joseph had taken out a second mortgage on the house. I confronted Jake with this and he said there was nothing we could say about it. That was the way it was. Jake had an accident at work, he fell from the roof of a shed and broke his left leg in four places. It was a bad break and after the cast was taken off he walked with a pronounced limp. His security business went under and he went to work for an old friend of his selling used cars. On his way to lunch one afternoon, driving one of the cars from the lot, Jake was rear-ended by another car and landed in the hospital. The accident turned out to have been Jake's fault: he'd not seen the other car approaching and had pulled out directly in front of it. Jake wound up with a bad back because of this calamity

159

and was out of work for three months. We had no health insurance and the money for the hospital bills came out of our pockets.

One disaster followed another. I became inured to Jake's failures and tried not to be overly upset by whatever happened. I knew he was trying to make a living as best he could. Jake loved me, he told me this often. He never said a word about the weight I'd gained, and he was kind to and supportive of Molly. She cared deeply for Jake and he felt as if she were his own daughter. Time passed faster than I realized, and one Christmas day it was Jake's and my tenth anniversary. It was all pretty silly, wasn't it? I said to Jake. "What's silly?" he asked. "Life," I said. "It doesn't make any sense to me." Jake came over and kissed me. "I know things haven't been so good lately, Peg," he said. "But I've got a new idea. Everything will work out. Just don't worry about it."

The summer she graduated from high school Molly and a girlfriend of hers took a trip to California to see Jimmy and explore the west coast. On the way back to Wisconsin they stayed with the girlfriend's relatives in Tucson, Arizona. Molly loved Tucson, she told me; she wanted to live there and go to school at the University of Arizona. Jake and I could not afford to pay for her college expenses, and neither could—or would—Andy, but Molly said she would work for a year and establish residency in the state. She could then matriculate at the university for much less than it would cost were she an out-of-state student. I knew that Molly's health would improve if she lived down there so I agreed to let her go, and convinced Jake that it was the wisest thing to do.

So Molly left me alone with Jake in Deer Run. I was happy for her and she was excited about being on her own. Molly got a job in a restaurant near the university and started putting money away for her schooling. I was proud of her and sad that I couldn't be of more help.

By this time Jake had become something of a persona non grata around Deer Run and in Madison. He managed to eke out a living selling cars for his friend Ernie Lloyd, but then Ernie got arrested in a stolen license plate scam and Jake was out of a job again. Our debts began to pile up, Jake couldn't find work, and then Joseph told him that the note on the house was due. If we wanted to keep the house, Joseph said, Jake would have to come up with the

161

payment. Joseph just could not carry us any longer, he said. If we couldn't pay we'd have to sell the house.

The thought of selling the house hit me very hard. Times had not been easy but I'd enjoyed living in Deer Run. I liked planting peas and corn and tomatoes every spring, tending the garden and befriending the raccoon that lived under our back porch for many years. We had nice neighbors, the Olsons and Webers and Jensens, practical, unpretentious, small town folks who were always bringing over home-made coffee cakes and other little presents for no reason other than they were good people who liked me. I would miss these friends, with none of whom had I ever had any difficulty. I had enjoyed seeing Molly grow up with their children, living where she could ride her bicycle out in the cornfields, in the country, not having to be in the midst of traffic in a crowded, smelly city. The schools were good here, Molly had gotten a good education, and I was grateful for that.

I asked Jake if he would to go his older brother, Bill, and see if he wouldn't rehire him at LaPointe Steel, but Jake absolutely refused. He wouldn't crawl to Bill, he said; going to Joseph for help had been bad enough. We'd sell the house and leave town, said Jake. "I've been here my whole life," he told me. "Let's go someplace else, start over. I know a guy in San Diego," Jake said. "An old Navy buddy who's a pilot for a private airline. I'll write to him and tell him we're coming out." "We can't just run away to San Diego," I said. "That doesn't make any sense." "Why not?" Jake asked. "There's nothing left for me here. You can stay if you want, Peg, but I'm leaving. I'm a dead man in this place."

Joseph had no trouble unloading the house; it was in good condition and was in an excellent neighborhood. Joseph gave us two thousand dollars from the sale. Jake owed him so much money that he would have béen justified in not giving us anything. I was heartbroken. My home was gone, we were in the street with a few bucks and no real prospects.

Jake borrowed a truck from a friend and loaded all of our belongings into it. I had carefully packed my mother's antiques, her oriental rugs; they were all I had left in the world. I was sick, tired and depressed. I'd saved five hundred dollars from my job in the insurance office. I closed my account at the bank and sent two hundred dollars to Molly in Tucson, the rest I stuck in my pocket. Jake told me to drive our station wagon and handed me a piece of paper with an address in San Diego on it. He was grinning from ear to ear like a madman. "I'll drive the truck and meet you there," Jake said. "You'll see, everything will be different once we get to California. We'll be closer to Molly and Jimmy. We'll have a new life there." Jake kissed me, climbed into the truck and started it up.

$\mathbf{T}$here I was, a fat old lady driving an old station wagon loaded with suitcases and cardboard boxes across Iowa or Nebraska or wherever I was when the thought hit me: "What am I doing?" I said out loud to myself, "I don't know what I'm doing!"

My house was gone, my little house that I'd worked so hard in and around for so many years. The money I'd had was long gone, poured down the drain by two good-for-nothing husbands. How could I have been so stupid? I thought. I'd blown my life, and it wasn't likely that I'd get another chance. I didn't see that I deserved one, either. Maybe I was better off being a gypsy. I'd trusted the wrong people, that's all, and I was paying the price. I felt sorry for myself and I disliked the feeling. It wasn't as if I'd started out with nothing. I'd never lived in a slum, never gone begging or been thrown into a concentration camp. What did I have to complain about?

Driving across the country I had plenty of time to think. I thought of the time Jimmy was born, when I'd received such grand bouquets from all of Rudy's hoodlum friends. One of them had sent an orchid tree that I especially liked. I was so well taken care of in those days. All I had to do was ask Rudy and I could have anything, anything except the freedom to live as I wanted. I remembered the times I'd walk into some store, I'd be looking at something, and a couple of boys would come in and say, "Hiya Peg. Do you want that?" The next thing I knew a saleslady would

164

be wrapping it up for me. I'd protest, try to refuse, but they'd say, "It's just a little present, Peggy. Take it, it's nothing." And I would always smile and say thank you very much.

I'd had a high old time in New York, running around with counts and princes; with Rudy and other boyfriends in Jamaica, Cuba, Mexico, Hawaii and Florida. I'd had a great time, really. And now I was poking along the highway to nowhere I knew like Ma Joad. I thought, this too shall pass. But meanwhile my life was passing. I was old, my looks were gone. No more long, billowy, chestnut red hair; it was gray.

Across the street from Rudy's store had been a lovely old building, long since torn down, that housed a masseuse and a hair dresser that I used to frequent. Inga had a string of girls that she employed as masseuses for men on an appointment only basis, but Inga was a legitimate masseuse and I loved to go over to her place a couple of times a week and have a massage and get my hair done. She would tell me hilarious stories about the customers her girls entertained, what they wanted and what they did, and I really enjoyed it all. Upstairs on the third floor lived a lovely old couple who dealt in rare books; they had every history book imaginable. I became very friendly with them and their two Siamese cats, which they had trained to use the regular toilet in the bathroom. Inga and this couple and I would sit around in the late afternoon and have tea or coffee. I liked being with them, getting away from Rudy's crowd, the so-called celebrities and syndicate characters with their tough guy talk. As I drove I wondered what had happened to Inga and the old couple, if they were still alive. There had been so many people in my life, they'd come and gone so quickly.

I mainly thought about my children. The one reason I was glad to be going to San Diego was that I would be closer to them. Both Molly and Jimmy were hard-working kids, I admired them. Molly would be attending the University of Arizona soon and could come to see me on her vacations, I wasn't so far away now. And it would be easy to travel up the coast to San Francisco to visit

Jimmy. Ever since he'd lived in England I had told him that one of the things I wanted to do before I died was to go on a walking tour of Scotland. Jimmy said he would take me and I liked reminding him about it. One of these days, I'd tell him, we're really going to go. When Jimmy had been a little boy and my mother was sick in bed with a bad heart, he'd say to her, "When you get well, Nanny, we're going to have a race. We'll run from the front of the house to the fence in the backyard." Rose would always smile at Jimmy when he said this. "Yes," she'd say, "as soon as I'm well," knowing she never would be. I intended to take that walking trip in Scotland, with or without Jimmy. I didn't know if by going to California I was getting any closer to my tour of Scotland, but, strangely enough, it seemed to me that I was.

$\mathbf{B}$y the time I got to San Diego I looked like a wreck. I expected sunshine and warmth but it was a cold and rainy April day. I stopped in a gas station and the attendant supplied directions to the address Jake had given me back in Deer Run, the home of his Navy pal, Jed Day. Jed was there and he gave me a nice welcome. He was afraid that something might have happened to me. He'd been expecting me to arrive for two days. Jake had been calling him from along the way; he'd phoned last night from Flagstaff. I told Jed that I'd taken my time. There was no hurry when you didn't know where you were going, was there?

Jake showed up the next night, exhausted, but smiling. He and Jed had only seen each other twice since their Navy pilot days so they had a pleasant little reunion. I just sat and half-listened to their conversation. We went out to dinner and Jed told Jake that he'd been scouting out job leads for him. He was certain that Jake would find something before too long. The next morning Jed drove us around, showing us the scenery. I'd had quite enough of scenery for the time being and could easily have done without the tour, but Jake was very animated and so positive about everything that I didn't want to dampen his enthusiasm. He was overjoyed to be so far away from Deer Run and Madison. Jake was convinced that San Diego was his Elysium.

That afternoon we rented a small, one-bedroom apartment near the ocean and moved most of our belongings into it. The rest we stored in a nearby warehouse. I hadn't seen Jake so happy since we were first married, and his optimism was infectious. Maybe we will make it, I thought that night in our new apartment. As long as we have our health, I figured, we have a chance.

After we were all moved in Jake told me that he had to go back to Deer Run, to return the truck he'd borrowed. "But I'll be back in a week," he said, "and with more money. I've got a few things to clear up in Madison. Now Peg . . . " I knew what he was about to say so I snapped, "Please don't tell me not to worry, Jake. I'll scream if you do." Jake laughed. "Okay, I won't," he said. "Just take this and take care of yourself until I get back. I'll let you know when I'm flying in." Jake handed me a roll of bills, most of what was left of the two thousand dollars Joseph had given us from the sale of the house.

I worked hard in the apartment while Jake was gone, fixing it up. I had a telephone installed and started to feel a little better. Jed came by a few days later and told me Jake had called him and said that he would be a little longer in Wisconsin than he'd thought. He was staying at a motel in Madison and I called him that night. Everything was fine, Jake said. A fellow owed him some money and as soon as he collected it he would be on the first flight to San Diego. I had my doubts but Jake turned out to be true to his word. Four days later he showed up with an extra thousand dollars. We didn't have much of a stake, he admitted, but it would be enough until he found a job.

The weather improved and my spirits improved with it. Everything seemed much brighter than it had in Deer Run, and I loved being on the ocean. The cost of living was higher than in Wisconsin, however, and when after two weeks Jake still had not found work, I began to worry. I spotted a Help Wanted sign in the window of a liquor store near our apartment and decided to apply for a job myself, without telling Jake. To my surprise, I was hired on the spot. The wages weren't great, but it was something.

When I told Jake about it he got angry and said he wouldn't let me work in a liquor store. "What do you mean?" I said. "It's just a clerk's job. And besides, I know all about the liquor business from when I was married to Rudy. He sold liquor in his drugstore." Jake tried to argue me out of taking the job but I wouldn't back down. I told him that as soon as he got a job somewhere and was making enough money to support us both I'd quit. That calmed him down and settled things for the moment.

I didn't mind the work at the liquor store. At first it bothered me to be on my feet all day behind the counter. There was a stool to sit on but it was a busy place and there were rarely lulls of any long duration. I got used to the routine, though, and soon I was doing fine. Every day I prayed that no one would pull a gun and stick me up. I'd had enough of that kind of thing. But the owner assured me that this was a good area. He'd only been robbed once in twelve years, he said, and that had been an after hours, inside job.

Jake went to work after about two months of searching. A car dealer needed a man to drive new Cadillacs to Mexico City. All he had to do, Jake said, was drive the car to Mexico, drop it off at a certain location, and fly back to San Diego. I told him that I'd never heard of any job like that, it had to be some kind of illegal deal. "I don't care if it is, Peggy," said Jake. "As long as I don't know the details I'll be all right. Besides, nobody else is knocking down the door to offer me a job." I told him that unless he *did* know all the details he'd probably get into more trouble than he would otherwise, but Jake wouldn't listen. He didn't like the idea of my being the only one working, I understood that, and he promised to keep looking for something else.

I had some spending money from my job. I really couldn't save very much, we were only making it from week to week, but I relaxed. I lost weight and sat in the sun, swam in the ocean. Jake was gone for days at a time to Mexico and I found that I didn't mind being alone. It was like when I was a child in the house in Prairie Park, when I liked to sit in the nook and read. I had no desire to make new friends, not the way I had in Deer Run. I kept

169

to myself and read books. I read good books, ones I'd meant all my life to read: *Madame Bovary, The Brothers Karamazov*, Proust, Faulkner. After work I'd haunt the library.

Jed Day called me one evening to ask how I was doing. I told him that we were getting by, that I was well. Jed said he'd heard that Jake was working for the Dragulis brothers and wanted to know if it was true. I told him I'd never heard of the Dragulis brothers. Who were they? "Just some guys I don't think Jake ought to be messing around with," Jed said. "Ask him about it, will you?" I asked Jed why he didn't ask Jake himself. "I would," he said, "but I can't ever get hold of him."

Jake was out of town when Jed called so the next day at the liquor store I asked Moe Dorfman, the owner, if he knew of anyone by the name of Dragulis. "Sure," he said, "Nick and Steve Dragulis. They own a couple of car dealerships downtown. I don't know them personally but they've been around for a while." Moe didn't offer any more information so I didn't push it. I decided to ask Jake about them when he got back from Mexico.

"They're right guys," Jake said on his return. "I've been doing a little work for them." "Then why did Jed say that you shouldn't be messing around with them?" I asked. "I don't know," said Jake. "Just what do you do for Nick and Steve Dragulis, Jake? I want to know. What's in those cars you drive down there, anyway? Drugs?" "No more cars, Peg," Jake said. "We're moving heavy machinery now to Tijuana. It's easy. All we have to do is pay the *mordidas* all around, the bribes." "What do they pay you for your part in the deal?" I asked. "I haven't seen you bringing home any big checks lately." "It's coming, Peg, it's coming. These things take time to set up properly. I'm going back over the border in a couple of days," said Jake. "I'll be able to tell you more about it after that."

*   *   *

170

Reading over what I've written, I'm hard put to come up with an easy answer. All I know is that I refuse to be a burden to my children. I can take care of myself, I'm sure of that much. I don't have to depend on Jake or anyone else. Regardless of what happens to him I'll be all right. Maybe the next time he comes back, or the time after that, I won't be here, I don't know. How foolish it is to assume that things will turn out for the best.

Andrew Partos

Barry Gifford was born in 1946 in Chicago, Illinois, and was raised there and in Florida. He has lived in London and San Francisco, among other places, and has worked as a merchant seaman, journalist, truck driver and musician. Mr. Gifford has been the recipient of an American Library Association Notable Book Award, a National Endowment for the Arts Fellowship in Creative Writing for Fiction, the Maxwell Perkins Award from P.F.N., and the P.E.N. Syndicated Fiction Prize. He lives in northern California.